To Jue

thank you for unleashing
my writing power

Lorraine xx

13:22

and other stories

Lorraine Forrest-Turner

I used to wonder why creative people felt the need to make such a big thing about thanking family, friends, colleagues, acquaintances, editors and complete strangers. But, having now joined the ranks of "grateful writer", I totally get it. When someone makes time to look at your work, and give you feedback on it, you really do need to say a massive thank you.

Many people have read (or listened to) stories in this book. I am hugely grateful to all of them. But I'd like to single out a special few.

To my friends at Slough Writers, thank you for giving me the encouragement I needed to keep me writing and the feedback I wanted to make it better. To my daughter Terri, thank you for overcoming the fear of "reading embarrassing stuff written by my mother" and giving me another perspective on life. And to my husband Andy, thank you for bolstering my fragile ego, being my diligent proofreader and never losing faith in me – even after reading some pretty awful early drafts.

Contents

13:22 and other stories

13:22

Claire's story

I'd never known the A27 this clear on a Saturday, especially not in August. We were going to get to the station far too early and have to wait ages for the train.

"Looks like we needn't have left so early, after all," I ventured. Dad gave me one of his tight-lipped smiles, leaving me to wonder if he was pleased to be proved right or annoyed at being dragged away from his mulching earlier than necessary. "I know we left really early but I'm really worried about – "

"Claire, you don't have to go through with this, you know. You don't have to put your life at risk. We can still turn back."

I breathed deeply and forced myself to say nothing. The last thing I wanted was another fight. I was getting on the train, going to London and doing something wonderful for someone else. You'd think he of all people would have been proud of me.

"I am worried about missing the train," I said, stressing each syllable evenly. "I am not worried about a routine procedure."

I could see his mouth beginning to form the same argument he'd been making for the last two weeks. But he stopped himself and we drove on in silence.

Dad had been annoyed with my decision to become a donor from day one. Four years earlier, a representative from Anthony Nolan had given a talk at Uni and I'd gone home that weekend excited about telling Dad I was going to register.

Mum had died of blood cancer when I was two and I'd thought Dad would have been delighted. I couldn't have been more wrong. Not only was he not happy about my decision, he refused to even talk about it.

It was only when I'd got the call two weeks ago (saying I was a match and asking me to go for further tests) that he began to talk.

First, he said I shouldn't put my new job at risk. I'd only started as a graduate trainee a month ago and I shouldn't be expecting time off already.

I explained that the company was really supportive, and that my boss was dead proud of me, but Dad dismissed it as "political correctness". Then, when I went to London for the tests, he said the needles could be contaminated and I could get blood poisoning.

No amount of showing him websites, letters and testimonials had any effect. Finally, he came out with the classic, "Don't you realise that some people don't even make it through a general anaesthetic?"

I made the mistake of laughing at that and he went berserk. I'd never seen him that angry. He was ranting like a demon. He accused me of not loving him, of playing God, of being selfish, of risking my life for a complete stranger. I'd burst into tears and ran out of the house. I hadn't stopped to pick up my bag or my phone so once I'd calmed down slightly, I walked round to my aunt Lesley's house a few miles away.

I don't want to hurt Dad, I told her between sobs and sips of tea. I loved him more than anything or anyone. But if my spending a day or two in hospital could save someone's life – save some other kid from growing up without a mum – I had to do it. Surely he'd come round eventually, wouldn't he?

Lesley, my mum's sister, wasn't so sure. She thought it was a guilt thing. She said Dad had never forgiven himself for letting my mum undergo chemo. He'd let her go through all that suffering, he'd say, only to lose her anyway. Now, there was a chance he'd lose me. Or rather, that's what he'd convinced himself.

Now, as the clock on the dashboard read 13.22, I figured we'd be in Brighton in about 20 minutes. I had to try again. I looked over at him. It was hard to know what he was thinking. He was a good driver and rarely spoke at the best of times. This probably wasn't the best place, but it really was the only time.

"Dad… I'm… You didn't… I could have got the bus… Thank you for giving me a lift." I could see him bite his bottom lip and my eyes immediately filled with tears. Why was I doing this to him?

9

"Well… we don't want you missing that train, do we?"

I reached over to touch his knee, to show him how grateful I was, how much I loved him, but his arm shot out across my body, and I pulled back instantly. He was looking in his rear view mirror, his eyes wide with surprise. "What the hell is that?" he said. "Wow. That gave me a shock."

I'm immediately looked behind me as Dad and the other cars around us slowed down. It was hard to make out exactly what it was or where it was coming from but there seemed to be a huge cloud of thick black smoke and massive dark red flames over towards the Shoreham air show we'd passed a few moments earlier.

"Looks like a lorry has crashed or something," Dad said, a little calmer now. "Just as well we left early, eh? We wouldn't have wanted to have got caught up in all that and have you miss that important appointment."

***

Hazel's story

She was fussing. She knew she was fussing. But if she couldn't make a fuss over James coming home, what could she make a fuss over?

Robert was hovering. He was doing his 'what would you like me to do' thing when what she really wanted him to do was take some flipping initiative and think for himself. Couldn't he see the rubbish by the back door, the washing basket in the living room, the state of the kitchen floor, for heaven's sake!

He finished checking his Facebook status (if one ever could 'finish' social media) and put his phone down. "Is there anything you'd like me to do?" he asked. Hazel resisted the urge to bark "isn't it obvious?" and asked him to take the rubbish out.

It was the end of August. She hadn't seen her son since Christmas, and she wanted to 'do everything' before he got here so she could sit down and relax for once. It felt that every time James came home, she spent the whole time in the kitchen. She'd hear him and Robert in the lounge, watching TV, laughing at some stupid thing on Dave, and she'd feel a flush of happiness tinged with jealousy. Why wasn't she in there? He was her son, after all.

Robert was a brilliant stepfather. He'd never tried to be anything more than a stepfather. James's dad, Paul, was still very much on the scene and in Robert's books, the last thing James needed was another father giving him unwanted (and often, in Robert's opinion, unsound) advice. He'd plumped for the friend, the confidante, the wiser older man. He loved Hazel as much as James did and he didn't want to compete on any level.

Hazel had left James's dad when James was three. She should have left him years earlier, she should never have got involved with him in the first place, but as she later told her parents, you don't leave your husband because your marriage is bad; you stay because it's not bad enough.

She still remembered the utter delight she felt on that first night in her tiny rented flat. She had no money, no childcare facilities, no idea how she'd cope as a single mum, but her little boy was safely asleep in the next room, she was alone in what felt like an enormous double bed and no-one was going to start questioning her on why she'd bought that particular brand of soap powder, why she was wearing that old jumper, why she only wore make-up when she went out to work, why she was letting James sleep so late, why she hadn't taken him to the doctor yet... It was going to take a while to stop hearing Paul's voice in her head.

The first year or so after the break-up was tough. Paul swung back and forth from being incredibly understanding to sheer bloody-minded. But they gradually settled into a routine and Hazel braved the occasional date on the nights James stayed at Paul's.

She met Robert at a school reunion. He seemed to remember her far more than she remembered him, but they hit it off immediately and the following day she found herself unable to think of much else.

Juggling the demands of work, James and Robert proved to be almost as difficult as her marriage to Paul and she tried several times to end her relationship with Robert. It was her mother who'd made her think differently.

"Don't make the same mistake I did, love," her mother had said one afternoon as they sat watching the now five-year-old James poking a dead crab with his spade. "Kids are important, but a man isn't going to play second fiddle forever."

Hazel had always blamed her father for the break-up of her parents' marriage. Was her mother now implying that her neglect was partly to blame?

Hazel and James moved in with Robert two days before James's sixth birthday. Like the previous big change in her life, it wasn't easy. But Robert was patient, understanding and only occasionally frustrated with James's jealousy and unreasonable behaviour.

Gradually, James came to realise that Robert was no threat, his own father was a "waste of space", and he was happy in his new domestic arrangement.

Now, 20 years on, Paul was married with a young family and James shared what little free time he had relatively equally between both sets of parents – which meant Hazel saw far less of him than she'd like.

"What time is it?" she asked as Robert came back into the kitchen. He looked puzzled, eyed the clock on the wall, the one on the cooker and the one on the heating system before saying "about twenty past one".

"No, I need the exact time." Hazel was peering into the dark oven, wishing Robert had fixed the wretched bulb when she'd asked him. Who attempted soufflés without a light in the oven? "If I'd wanted a rough time, I'd have looked at one of the three clocks we have in here. I need an exact time. I'm doing a test run on a soufflé."

Robert picked up his phone. "At the third stroke, it will be 13.22 and 6 seconds."

"Shouldn't he be here by now?" she asked, wondering if she should open the oven door. "What time did he say he was setting off?"

"Around 11.00, I think. He's probably got held up in traffic. There's an air show at Shoreham today. That often creates a back log."

"Give him a call. I need an accurate ETA. Why on earth did I decide to make soufflés today? And why can't we get this flipping light fixed!"

Robert hit "James" on his phone and waited for it to go voice mail. James never answered his phone. "It's gone to voice mail."

"Then leave a message."

"Hello son. Mum's wondering what time you're getting here as she's doing soufflés and… Sorry… she's saying something… What?"

"Just ask him to call!"

"Just give us a call, son. No rush. Lots of love."

"Ruined!" Hazel flung the sunken soufflé onto the hob and Robert found an excuse to get out of the kitchen.

Her attention now turned to the Coronation Chicken. Had it been out of the fridge too long? She had taken it out at 12.00 so it would be more flavoursome at room temperature. What on earth was keeping James?

She found Robert asleep in front of the TV. Oh, to be a man, she thought. She picked up the remote to turn the TV off when something caught her eye.

Over what looked like amateur footage of an aircraft tumbling to the ground, a voice was saying, "News has just come in of a Hawker Hunter jet from the Shoreham air show crashing into the A27. It is believed that several people may have been killed instantly…" the voice continued under the shrill ringing in Hazel's ears.

"Robert… Robert… What road does James take?"

"Oh. Sorry love. I must have dropped off. Is James here?" Robert looked at his wife's face and got to his feet. "Sweetheart. Sweetheart, what's wrong?"

Hazel continued to gaze at the television as Robert's mobile rang from the kitchen.

***

Jake's story

His first thought as he woke was 'thank god, I'm not dead', swiftly followed by 'oh my god, please let me die'.

Surely this feeling of utter wretchedness was more than a hangover. Nothing short of a brain tumour could produce this much pain. And what the hell was that rising in his stomach. Shit, he was going to...

Jake hadn't been sick in bed since he was five. Where was his mum when he needed her? The stench was making him heave and he managed to get himself to the toilet before throwing up again. He was going to kill Andy Marston when he saw him. Assuming, that is, he'd live long enough to do it.

Bed stripped, sheets in washing machine and a bacon sandwich on the breakfast bar, Jake was convinced he was actually getting worse. He knew he needed to eat – or at least drink something – but even a sip of water was making him wretch. What the hell was in those shots?

He grabbed the duvet, gave it a quick sniff (only a slight hint of vomit) and lay on the sofa. Hopefully, Football Focus would take his mind off death.

He'd just got settled into a position where his headache was reduced to an agonising throb when he heard his phone ringing upstairs. He let it ring.

After his mobile rang and stopped four times, the landline burst into action. It was so long since anyone rang the landline, he physically jumped. Jesus, someone was keen to talk!

He moved slowly, hoping it would stop before he got to it. It didn't. He answered and made a sound vaguely resembling "y'all".

"Jake, me best bro. How the fuck are you?" It was Dan, Jake's self-appointed line manager.

"Shit. I'm worse than shit. I'm liquidised shit in vomit."

"Yeah. Great. Me too."

Just a year older than Jake and with the courier company they both worked for precisely one week longer, Dan had taken it upon himself to 'manage the new kid'. That was two years ago. Despite repeatedly telling Dan "you're not my boss", Dan continued to emotionally blackmail, bully and generally cajole Jake into doing stuff nobody else wanted to do.

"Look Jake. I need you to do something for me."

"It's Saturday. It's my weekend off. And I don't work for you." Feeling like death had given Jake a new lease of life.

"Yeah, yeah. Whatever. We've got to get a delivery to The Three Monkeys in Portsmouth by 2.00 and you're the only one who can do it."

What Jake should have done at that point was hang up. At the very least, he should have said "not my problem, mate". So why the hell did he hear himself saying, "Why can't you go?"

"It's my sister's wedding today! Jesus, Jake. How could you have forgotten? She's spoken about nothing else for eighteen months!"

It was indeed Dan's sister's wedding. How

could he have forgotten? She'd been in the office pretty much every day for the last month having at least one driver picking up or delivering flowers, dresses, shoes, favours (whatever they were) and umpteen other "crucially important things" for her Big Day. There were so many deliveries to so many addresses, Jake was convinced half of Hampshire was attending Dan's sister's wedding.

Jake made several feeble attempts to tell Dan where to stuff the delivery but, as always, Dan somehow managed to convince Jake that it would take no time at all, would go down really well at his six-monthly review, would be worth an extra pony or two in his pay packet and win him great favour with the beautiful barmaid, Donna.

The vision of Donna pulling a pint at The Three Monkeys was enough to bring a bit of colour to Jake's face. Maybe getting out and thinking of something else was what he needed?

He pulled on last night's jeans and t-shirt, made a half-hearted attempt to brush his teeth and stopped in at the garage to stock up on a bottle of fat Coke, a packet of Monster Munch and a Ginster's cheese pasty. A few miles later, the radio on full blast and the six paracetamols finally taking effect, Jake began to feel a little more human. He might even manage a pint from the delightful Donna.

The A27 was unusually quiet for a Saturday afternoon in August. Maybe Jake's sister had invited half of Hampshire to the wedding? He glanced at the clock. 13.22. He was going to get to The Three Monkeys long before 2.00. He was definitely feeling better. In fact, he was feeling pretty good. Yeah, he did the right thing getting out of the house. Dan had done him a great big favour.

It came from nowhere. No vision. No sound. No smell. Nothing. Suddenly, it was there. Right in front of him. In the nanosecond it took him to think "what the fuck is that", the Hawker Hunter jet burst into flames and Jake watched as the wedding Daimler that should have been picking up Dan's sister ploughed straight into it. Jake rammed on his brakes, the van swung 360 degrees and for the second time that day, he thanked god he wasn't dead.

Beetroot tears

I walk from room to room. All that's left is a few heavy items of furniture remain.

Exactly 23 weeks since Dad left our family home for the last time, the house has gradually been cleared of clothes and books and shoes and golf clubs and weed killer and rusty tins and dusty ornaments. The best, the most nostalgic items, taken home by family to keep safe for the next generation. The useful given to charity. The majority thrown into black bags and tossed into overflowing communal bins. 23 weeks since we lost Dad. Five years and five months since we lost Mum. But the house still resonates with their presence.

I look out of windows, touch carpets, smell wallpaper, and soak in 54 years for the very last time. "We were happy here," I say to the ghosts. "Most of the time." And then, just as I turn to pick up my handbag from the kitchen worktop, I see them. Two tiny beetroot tears just as I'd seen that night 49 years ago.

***

"Lucy," Mum said, putting a piece of bacon and egg pie on my plate. "Tell your brother his supper's getting cold."

"John!" I yelled, picking at some pastry on the baking tray. "Your supper's getting cold!"

"Lucy! That was right in my ear!" Mum moved the baking tray out of my reach. "I meant you to go upstairs and tell him."

I took my plate to the table. Dad was in his place in the corner, the Evening Express safely under his bum. He'd always sit on the paper during meals to ensure ownership.

"John!" Mum shouted from the foot of the stairs. "I'm not telling you again!"

"Just leave him," Dad said, putting a forkful of pie in his mouth. "He'll… mumble… enough… mumble… starving." Which I took to mean 'he'll come down soon enough if he's starving'. My brother spent a lot of time in his room these days. I tried not to imagine why.

"Are there any beans?" I asked, looking at my plate. "It's a bit dry without beans."

Mum sat next to Dad and rubbed her head. She looked tired. "We've run out."

"We've got some beetroot," I suggested.

"Just eat it as it is!" Dad spat a bi of pastry onto his chin. "It's too much trouble to get the jar out the cupboard."

'Too much trouble' was Dad's response to pretty much anything. Can I get a lift to Sasha's? 'Too much trouble to get the car out.' Out of what, I was never sure. We didn't have a garage or even a driveway. Can I eat my supper in the living room? 'Too much trouble to take everything in there.' Everything being my plate.

I eyed the cupboard behind Dad and

reasoned it wasn't 'too much trouble' if I acted quickly. But before I had a chance to move, John came in, sat down and blocked my exit. He had a piece of blood-stained tissue stuck to his chin.

"Can I look at the paper, Dad?" John asked.

"I'm in… mumble… of reading it."

I looked at John. He looked at the Evening Express under Dad's bum then gave me a knowing look. "What? With your bum?" we thought in unison. It had been our running gag for years. Never failed to make us smile.

Dad and John argued about some disallowed goal on Saturday, and I pushed my pie around my plate. I could see Mum tense up, but I was determined to continue my bid for beetroot.

"It's too dry without beetroot," I ventured, standing up.

"Sit down, Lucy!" Dad snapped. "It's right at the back of the cupboard and I'm not getting up again."

"You don't have to get up," I braved. "I can lean over you."

With only a sideways glance from Mum and a grunt from Dad, I took my chance, leant forward and manoeuvred my way around him. I managed to open the cupboard door far enough to reach inside but couldn't quite get to the jar. So, I leant in a bit further, pressing up against John and knocking the piece of tissue off his chin.

John yelled, Mum shouted, Dad swore, and I dropped the jar straight onto the kitchen table.

Fortunately, it didn't break.

Unfortunately, the last person who'd used it (probably me) hadn't put the lid back on properly. Burgundy coloured vinegar splatted everywhere. And I mean, everywhere. Over the table, up the walls and into the ridges of the new tongue-and-groove-beech-effect wall paneling.

"Now look what you've done!"

"You eejit!"

"What did I say? Eh? What did I say?"

"Hand me that cloth."

"Just leave it!"

"It wasn't my fault."

"Leave it! Leave it alone!" Dad's voice bellowed through the chaos. "Just sit down and eat your supper!" We sat down. "Your mother works hard enough without you two creating nothing but trouble!"

"But I…" John cut in.

"If I hear one more word out of either of you," Dad hissed, "I'll take those plates and put the whole lot in the bin!"

John and I exchanged a knowing glance and Mum rubbed the side of her head.

We sat in silence.

It must have been torture for Mum, leaving all that mess everywhere. God, she'd have a hissy fit if you left your shoes in the hallway! But we all knew not to rattle Dad further, so we ate our dry (and now cold) pie as quickly as possible.

I'm never very good with tension at the best of times but all that suppressed rage and beetroot juice was giving me an overwhelming urge to giggle. I looked up at Mum, hoping her face would stifle my laughter. And that's when I noticed them. Two perfect burgundy 'tear drops' on the side of her nose. John had seen them too and shot me a look that said, "laugh now and we're both dead". This only made the giggle-urge stronger, so I stuffed my remaining pie into my mouth pronto.

After what felt like ages, Dad finally stood up and John and I leapt to our feet, delighted for once at the prospect of washing up. Anything to relieve the tension. Dad took the paper out from under his bum and headed towards the living room. Mum carried her and Dad's plate to the sink.

Suddenly, there was an almighty thud and Dad turned to shout: "What the hell are you two doing now?" Except he didn't get beyond "What the…" because he was staring at Mum, who was lying on the kitchen floor, her head inches from the bin, broken plates and pastry flakes at her feet.

She was thrashing about like a fish out of water. Her face twisted, her teeth locked, and a horrible deep growl was coming from her throat. She reminded me of the black dog tied up outside number 12.

I knew I was supposed to do something but all I could think was how undignified she looked lying there with her head next to the bin and two burgundy spots on the side of her nose.

"Do something!" John said, tugging at my arm. "You're good at science. Do something!"

Dad was motionless, his face frozen in a horrified stare. John looked terrified. "Do something!" he kept saying. "Do something!"

I'd got 19 out of 20 for my last chemistry test. But what had that to do with anything? Why was it my responsibility to do something?

"Why is she making that noise?" Dad spoke in a voice I'd never heard before.

And that was it. Suddenly, I was in command.

"John. Run over to Uncle George's and tell him Mum's having a fit. Dad, phone for an ambulance. Dial 999 and say my wife's collapsed and she's not breathing properly. Dad! Dad! Phone for an ambulance!"

John shot out the door, but Dad just stood there, gazing at Mum, his face scarier than the noises Mum was making.

I pushed past him, picked up the phone from the hall table and dialled 999. They answered quickly. I could hear my voice, steady and calm, describing the position Mum was in, how long she'd been out for, the sound she was making and whether she'd been sick or not. The woman on the

25

phone kept telling me how well I was doing, and I believed her. Maybe I'd get 'kid of the year' or something and I pictured myself being interviewed on the TV news.

I didn't want to go back into the kitchen after the call. I didn't want to see the growling dog and the motionless man. So, I sat on the stairs waiting for the ambulance and imagined telling everyone all about it at school tomorrow.

Then I remembered how it had happened. And the beetroot. And the spots on Mum's nose. And suddenly I didn't want to think about telling anyone or winning an award. I just wanted to be sick. Or die. Or both.

At some point, John must have come back with Uncle George. And Dad must have found his voice again because when the ambulance men came into the kitchen with their jokes and walkie talkies, Dad seemed fine.

I assumed it was Uncle George who'd put the blanket over Mum. And he must have cleaned her face too because when the men carried her out to the ambulance, I noticed the two burgundy spots had gone.

Dad went in the ambulance with Mum. And John asked if he could go round to his girlfriend's house. Uncle George said yes and then helped me wash the dishes and clean up the beetroot mess. He must have thought Mum had knocked the jar over when she fell because he never asked me what happened.

When the kitchen was finally tidy, and all the evidence washed away, I just wanted to be on my own, so I lied about having homework to do. Uncle George me made promise to phone him at any time then he left, and the house was silent.

I sat on the stairs again, gazing into space and making bargains with God. The same God I didn't believe in because I was too grown up and too good at science.

"Please God, I'll do anything if you make Mum okay again. I'll stop asking Dad to do stuff that's too much trouble. I'll stop winding John up about squeezing his spots and spending so much time 'reading' in his room. And I'll stop... I'll stop... hating Mum. I'll stop hating her for having headaches and being ill all the time."

There. I'd said it. I'd admitted hating the way Mum was always ill. The way Dad fussed about her all the time. The way he snapped at me and John for watching TV, playing music, asking to have mates round. I hated them both for stopping us being kids.

Was that what the beetroot was all about? Did I really want it? Or was I just sick of being good?

Whatever it was, I was sick now. Sick with shame. I'd made Mum sit there in all that mess. Knowing what I was putting her through. Knowing how much she was suffering. "Please God. Please don't let her die."

At 9.48, Dad called. They were waiting on

the results of the lumbar puncture, but Mum was "sleeping nicely" and I mustn't worry myself.

I should have high-fived God. I should have been dancing round the kitchen. And I would have been, if I hadn't seen them.

The last two spots of evidence. On the wall behind Mum's seat. Two perfect burgundy tear drops. Just like the ones on the side of her nose.

I dropped to the floor and sobbed.

***

Now, 49 years on, I take one last look at my childhood home. I see Mum calling us down for supper, Dad sitting on the Evening Express and John disappearing when it's time to clear up. I see the perfectly shaped beetroot tears and I drop to the floor and sob.

Chinchilla rats at Machu Picchu

Alan usually paid little attention to the radio in the mornings. It would come on at 6.30 for an hour, the time he used to get up when he had a two-hour commute around the M25 each weekday morning. But working from home had given him an hour of dozing through Zoe Ball's breakfast show and a leisurely breakfast before squeezing into the cupboard under the stairs to face a barrage of emails and back-to-back Zoom meetings.

Only this morning, something the newsreader was saying cut into Alan's sleep. He opened one eye to see 7.03 on the digital clock and the empty space where Sarah may or may not have slept last night.

"Chinchilla rats have re-emerged at Machu Picchu," she reported. "During lockdown, the rather timid arboreal rat, which is the size of a cat and looks like a fluffy dormouse, has reappeared near Peru's most visited destination. Scientists believe the lack of the usual 2,500 visitors a day in peak season has tempted the native rodent back to the World Heritage Site. Cameras installed in 2016 have shown…"

Alan made a mental note to check out the story on the Radio 2 website later and attempted to return to his dream about being on stage on with Phil Collins. But the sound of Sarah in the shower and the dryness of the bedroom (Sarah had refused to open a window during lockdown) forced him to get up.

"They've found chinchilla rats at Machu Picchu," he advised Sarah a little later as she entered the kitchen, towel drying her hair.

"Don't get toast crumbs on that worktop," she said, getting a side plate out of the cupboard. "Will they put poison down?"

Alan had long stopped wondering why it was wrong to eat toast in the kitchen but okay to towel dry hair. During their 40 plus years together, he had learnt that just about everything he did in the house was wrong. If he didn't put the dishwasher on, Sarah accused him of being lazy. If he did, she complained he stacked it badly. The same went for making beds, putting away shopping, vacuuming the carpets, taking towels out of the airing cupboard and a hundred other domestic normalities that he somehow managed to "make twice as bad".

"Poison?" he dared to ask.

"For the rats."

He began to explain how the chinchilla rats were an endangered species – actually believed to have died out altogether – but Sarah had already left the kitchen, muttering something about the amount of washing she was having to do now that he was at home every day. Even by Sarah's standards, that one made no sense whatsoever.

While Alan was delighted not to be sitting on the M25 twice a day, five days a week, being stuck at home 24 hours a day, seven days a week was driving him and Sarah slowly insane.

He'd never thought of theirs as a great marriage. They weren't 'best buddies' as some of his colleagues referred to their other halves. Neither did they share the same hobbies or interests. In fairness, few people these days shared his passion for Phil Collins. But their marriage had been tolerable. More than tolerable. They rarely argued. Unless one considered being constantly told he was doing something wrong as arguing. In fact, they rarely even spoke to one another. There was always so much else to do. Alan left for work early, got back late, played golf most weekends, and Sarah was always at, or preparing for, some important meeting or other.

When they were at home, the house was always packed with other people. Their grandchildren had outgrown spending summers and weekends at the house, but, over the years, they seemed to have accumulated a wide circle of acquaintances. On Sarah's insistence, there was always a regular gathering at their house. There had been invitations to go elsewhere but Sarah preferred to eat and serve her own food than dine at restaurants or other people's houses, where, in Sarah's opinion the quality was customarily inferior.

All in all, the only time they were every actually alone together was last thing at night and first thing in the morning. Sarah usually got into bed around the same time as Alan, but his snoring invariably drove her into the spare room at some point during the night. Naturally, marital relations were a thing of the past, and neither seemed too concerned about that.

Now, six weeks into lockdown, and shackled to one another 24 hours a day, their tolerable marriage had become anything but, and Alan was beginning to wonder which one of them would be first to kill the other.

"We're constantly under each other's feet," he'd complained to their daughter Gayle on the phone. "I'm at my desk – well, when I say 'desk', I mean the shelf in the cupboard under the stairs that Mum insists I use because I'm 'too loud' everywhere else – from about 8.00am until gone six but I do have to emerge at some point during the day. I wouldn't be surprised if she insisted I install a toilet and a fridge in there so I wouldn't need to come out at all."

Gayle had made sympathetic sounds, between shouting at the teenagers to leave some food in the fridge and go do some "goddamn revising", before announcing that he and Mum had a big enough house to keep out of each other's way and that they would just have to "suck it up like the rest of us".

Alan had to admit that he wasn't terribly good at "sucking it up". The forced isolation was bringing out the worst in him and instead of getting used to being with each other – or treating it as a "little holiday" as some of his colleagues and their families were doing – he and Sarah were barely remaining civil to one another.

"Do you want to kill us?" Sarah barked as she leant across Alan and slammed the kitchen window closed. Alan had forgotten that she wasn't styling her hair these days and was momentarily surprised to see her back downstairs so quickly.

"It's going to be 28 degrees later," Alan reasoned, discreetly wiping his sleeve over the wet circle he'd made on the breakfast bar with his coffee cup. "Plus, coronavirus can't come in through windows." He knew it was a pointless argument, but his irritability was making him braver. "It's not an airborne virus."

"So, I suppose all those key workers are wearing masks for the fun of it," Sarah said, eyeing the stain on his shirt. His attempt to cover up his misdemeanour had been in vain. She reached into the cupboard under the sink for Vanish and Flash and sprayed both of them at Alan and the worktop simultaneously. "You'll need to take that shirt off so I can wash it immediately. I'll never be able to shift that coffee stain otherwise. See. You're coughing already."

"That's because you're spraying a load of chemicals in my face!" Alan dutifully removed his shirt and handed it to Sarah. For a brief moment, she seemed to be looking at his torso. He sucked his stomach in. "The first thing I'm doing after lockdown is joining a gym. Your lemon drizzle cake is too good."

He half expected a lecture on "just because I make them doesn't mean you have to devour them" and was surprised to hear Sarah say, "You've

33

always managed to maintain a good physique."

The rest of the week passed with relatively little animosity. Sarah managed to secure a supermarket delivery slot and was positively buzzing at the prospect of stocking her much depleted store cupboard. And Alan took advantage of the good weather and several cancelled meetings to dig over the old vegetable patch and sow some courgette and beetroot seeds he'd found in a jar at the back of the shed.

That evening, after a particularly long session pulling out brambles, Alan felt physically tired but mentally exhilarated. So much so, he was torn between not setting Sarah off, by walking dirty clothes through the house, and deliberately getting earth on the carpet just for the hell of it. He settled on an easy life and removed his gardening clothes and boots before venturing inside for a shower.

He was surprised to see them exactly where he'd left them by the back door when he came downstairs 20 minutes later. Sarah would normally have had the boots in the garage and the clothes in the washing machine within minutes of him taking them off. He was even more surprised to see her outside sitting on the garden bench with a glass of white wine in her hand. It had barely gone 5pm.

"Which group are you Zooming with tonight?" Alan asked, making his way over to her. "I won't go online if you need the extra band-width."

"You can have it all to yourself," Sarah said,

raising her hand to shield her eyes from the sun. "I'm completely zoomed out. If I have to stare at one more 'strategically placed bookcase' while shouting 'unmute yourself', I swear, I will tear my hair out."

"Oh, don't do that," Alan said, without thinking. "It looks really nice." If Alan didn't know better, he would have sworn he saw a slight blush creep over Sarah's cheek as she pushed back her wilder than usual hair and said there was no point in tidying herself up if no-one was going to see her. Alan took the conversation back to safer ground and said, "I might do that trivia quiz that the groundsman at the club is hosting on Facebook. You can join me if you like. I could use your knowledge on food and drink."

"No, thank you," Sarah said, getting up. "I've been finding it hard to sleep in this heat. I might just watch some TV after dinner and have an early night." When she reached the back door, she picked up Alan's gardening clothes and sighed. Alan felt oddly disappointed.

They ate Sarah's splendid cheese and onion tart in as good as silence. Alan attempted a few compliments, but Sarah was insistent that the pastry was soggy and the filling dry. Who was Alan to argue? But she did seem grateful for his offer to clear up as she'd given herself a bit of headache having a glass of wine in the sun and would probably go and have a little lie down.

Alan did his best to stack the dishwasher both carefully and quietly then crept upstairs to make sure the bedroom door was closed. The last thing he needed was to disturb Sarah with raucous laughter from the online quiz. She was lying asleep on his side of the bed, the setting sun picking up the now silver and gold highlights in her hair.

While she complained that she desperately needed a visit to the hairdresser, he liked the softer, longer, touch-of-grey look. He also noted that he wasn't the only one who had "maintained a good physique". Seeing her stretched out on top of the duvet, wearing a white linen shirt and cropped denim jeans, Alan thought she looked as lovely as she did in her twenties.

After the quiz finished, Alan took a beer into the lounge, fully expecting to be told off for both having another and having it on the sofa. But Sarah didn't mention the beer. She sat very quietly listening to the news. The family of a 13 year-old boy dying of Covid-19 weren't being allowed to see him. It was only when he looked closer, he saw a single tear trickle down Sarah's cheek.

A few days later, thrilled that Asda had been able to send 500 grams of plain flour the night before, Sarah asked Alan if he wanted pancakes for breakfast. He waited to see if she was expecting him to do some chores as a trade-off; she usually did. But there didn't appear to be any provisos, so Alan accepted graciously.

"And I'm cutting your hair afterwards," she said, creating a well in the centre of the flour and beating the egg in. "The cul-de-sac is doing a socially-distanced front garden VE celebration on

Friday, and I want you to look respectable."

There would have been a time when Alan would have refused to have had his hair cut just because Sarah was insisting he had to. But lockdown had become wear-down, and he allowed himself to be seated at the dressing table mirror with an old bath towel around his neck and warm water sprayed onto his hair. Sarah held a comb in one hand, scissors in the other and a serious look on her face. She put the scissors in the pocket of her apron and lifted the back of Alan's hair with the comb. An electric sensation shot down his neck and Sarah pulled back instinctively. "It's okay," she said, misunderstanding Alan's response. "I used to cut the children's hair all the time when they were little." Alan couldn't remember the last time Sarah had touched him and for the third time in a matter of days, he experienced a feeling of tenderness towards his wife.

Several of the neighbours on VE day refused to believe that Alan hadn't broken lockdown rules and visited a professional hairdresser. "I wouldn't let my wife brush my hair, let alone cut it," Pete from number 3 bellowed across the close. "But I'd be very happy to let your missus loose on my head." Always one to dismiss praise, Sarah seemed to be enjoying the compliments and gave Alan what he was convinced was a cheeky wink.

Some hours (and several glasses of wine and beer) later, they made their way up to bed. "I looked them up on Google," Sarah said, removing her make-up. "They're really cute."

"Looked who up?" Alan asked, stifling a yawn.

"The chinchilla rats at Machu Pichu."

"Oh, yes… large… fluffy dormice…" Alan was finding it hard to keep his eyes open.

"It's surprising what can happen," Sarah said, getting into bed and placing a hand on Alan's leg, "when you leave the natives to their own devices."

Alan turned to his wife and touched her face gently. She responded with the lightest, most erotic kiss he'd ever experienced. Suddenly, it wasn't just the chinchilla rats who'd found their way back home.

Cuckoo

If there were such a thing as the perfect multi-family holiday villa, 'Casa Los Pinos' was it. Walking distance of the beach and Puerto Pollensa old town. Six bedrooms. Massive pool. Outdoor kitchen. And sufficient verandas to provide sun, shade or solitude when you'd had enough of everyone else.

"Move," I said. "You're blocking the sun." I wriggled to the right, but the shadow created by Martin's body was bigger than my sunbed.

"G&T?"

"Ah. That's different." I sat up. Martin handed me a tall glass, beaded with condensation. It rattled with US portions of ice. Such luxury.

"You're not burning, are you, Jenny? You've been out here for hours."

"I'm taking advantage of the peace. The kids will be back any – "

With precision timing, our 15-year-old son leapt out from nowhere, dive-bombed the pool and soaked both of us.

"Hey, Jacob!" Martin cried. "What have we said about – "

Three more youngsters appeared, the noise level grew 50 decibels and Martin and I retreated to the west-facing veranda.

"I'll give my girls a slap if you like," Linda

said, barely looking up from her book.

"They're just having fun," Martin said quickly, worried Linda might actually have meant it. "They're all getting on so well. Jacob loves having your girls around."

"Where's Ken?" I asked.

"Marinating the pork," Linda said, taking a long drag of her Marlboro.

"Oh," Martin said, clearly disappointed. "I thought I was cooking tonight. I've already – "

Linda sat up, closed her book, stubbed out her cigarette into the already full ashtray and muttered something about another beer. It took me a moment or two to realise it was a command and not an offer.

"Coming right up." Martin disappeared into the kitchen as happy as a puppy playing 'fetch'. Linda yelled to the kids to pipe down. And I took a large swig of gin.

Ken emerged from the kitchen wearing the 'six-pack' apron we'd bought for his last birthday. It was surprisingly realistic.

"You see what the kids are doing?" Ken asked, passing Linda a beer. "Whacking each other with pool noodles! Think I might go join them. Hey! Martin! Want to go wind up the youngsters?"

The men threw themselves into the pool. The girls squealed, and Linda and I laughed because that's what you do when you're a bit merry on a

Tuesday afternoon in Majorca.

***

"What dead animal is this?" Mandy, Ken and Linda's younger daughter, demanded. She prodded the expertly cooked pork and pulled a face only 14-year-old girls can pull.

"Pig!" Tilly shouted with delight, spearing another mouthful. I wasn't always proud of my daughter's behaviour, but I did admire her attitude to food.

"It's pork," reasoned their elder daughter, Alice. "It's delicious. It's falling off the bone."

"Bone?" Mandy shrieked. "What? An actual bone? Gross!"

"I'll have it." Jacob snatched the pork from Mandy's plate. Martin and I yelled, "No!" Ken said, "That'll teach you." Mandy burst into tears, and Linda burst into laughter.

Soothed by some left-over lunchtime pizza, Mandy joined the other kids in the outhouse where some feral kittens had taken up residence. Ken and Linda downed several cheap Spanish brandies. And Martin and I made a hasty retreat for some drunken, holiday sex.

***

I woke after 9.00 to an empty bed and the sound of Spanish radio playing outside. Raoul, the pool man, was late today. He'd usually been and gone by 8.00.

I poured myself a coffee from the cafetiere

in the kitchen and went outside. Half-empty cereal bowls and assorted beakers were abandoned on the table. A note from Martin read, "Taking the kids to the market. Back for lunch. Thanks for last night. Smiley face." I wallowed momentarily in the memory.

"You want fresh?" I turned to see a girl about Jacob's age. She was holding the pool net and looking impossibly beautiful. "Raoul, my cousin, hurt his back. I'm Sophie. You're Linda?"

"No. I'm Jenny. Linda's my friend. We're two families."

"You want fresh?"

"Fresh?"

"Coffee. You want me to make some fresh coffee?"

"Yes. No. Thank you. I never drink coffee at home. It's always tea first thing. But here, on holiday…I… well…" I was babbling. Something about this dazzling creature in the tiny bikini was very disconcerting. "Sorry about Raoul."

I was saved further embarrassment by the emergence of Ken. He greeted Sophie with a long "hel-low" reminiscent of those awful Leslie Phillips films.

Distracted by what Ken called 'practising his Spanish', Sophie was still with us when Martin and the kids turned up several hours later. The dive bombs that usually signalled their arrival were silenced at the sight of Sophie wiping down the sunbeds. Did she need to bend quite that low?

Jacob's voice dropped an octave. Tilly was speechless. Mandy gushed. Alice welcomed Sophie in surprisingly good Spanish. And Martin somehow managed to kiss me and put the shopping down without taking his eyes off the mesmerising beauty. Even Linda, who barely tolerated her own kids, seemed to find our cuckoo's presence an utter delight.

***

The invitation for Sophie to stay to dinner seemed to morph out of nowhere. She'd been there all day, why wouldn't she join us for something to eat?

I'd never known the kids spend more than half an hour at the table. But, tonight, no-one seemed in a hurry to go anywhere. Tilly and Alice listened avidly to Sophie's tales about the villa's previous residents. The men fell over themselves to pour Sophie a Coke every time her glass was empty, and Mandy, on seeing Sophie scoffing Martin's rosemary and garlic lamb, helped herself to a large plateful.

"Thought you didn't eat dead animals," Jacob pointed out. Mandy ignored him. As did Sophie, much to Jacob's disappointment.

It was only when I mentioned that it was getting rather late that anyone even considered how Sophie would get home.

"I will walk!" she said, gallantly.

"Walk?" everyone cried, followed by, "You can't", "I'll drive you", "You've had too much to drink", "I'll walk with you!"

"I'll call a taxi," I shouted.

"Good luck with that, Jenny." Linda poured herself a large Rioja. "There's only one taxi firm around here and you have to book them weeks ahead."

"She can stay in my room!" Tilly yelled. "I have a spare bed!" I had never seen Tilly so deliriously happy. She literally clapped her hands with glee. Glee!

All my attempts at reason – Sophie's family will be worried, she didn't have sleepwear, there was no spare bedding – were shot down with equally reasoned responses.

Sophie accepted graciously, retook her seat at the table and insisted Jacob tell her "absolutely everything" about English football. Both our son and daughter had reached new levels of ecstasy.

***

Having gone to bed relatively early, I'd expected to be first up. But when I crept into the kitchen around 8.00, I was staggered to see four teenagers and two adults sitting at the breakfast table behaving beautifully.

"Who's for some more?" asked Sophie, passing Ken a plate of perfectly poached eggs. Had it not been for the sight of Linda outside with a Marlboro Light in one hand and a large mug of coffee in the other, I'd have thought I'd woken up in a parallel universe.

By the end of the week, the cuckoo was well and truly settled in our nest.

The group dynamics we'd enjoyed before her arrival took on a whole new vibe. Jacob's boyish playfulness had been replaced with pathetic 'grown up' attempts to impress her. The three girls vied for her attention and approval. And the men became incoherent in her company. Even the unphased Linda appeared rattled.

"Is it just me?" Linda asked, watching Sophie rubbing suntan lotion into her pert bronze breasts. "Or do you think she's doing that deliberately?"

***

"Shotgun the front seat," Tilly cried, pushing her way ahead of the other girls. I'd volunteered to take them shopping. Naturally, Sophie came too.

"It's my turn," Mandy said. "You sat in the front on Tuesday."

"Yeah. But we only went to the market," Tilly pointed out. "You got the front for hours when we went to Formentor!" The ever sensible Alice suggested Sophie take the front seat so she could direct me to the mall.

The happy banter that had accompanied previous trips was now replaced by sulking. Mandy and Tilly refused to talk to each other, and Alice spent the whole journey glued to her mobile.

At the mall, Mandy grabbed one of Sophie's arms and Alice took the other. I tried to engage Tilly in conversation, but she only grunted monosyllabically. The sight of the three of them in fits of laughter ahead of us was tearing at her young heart.

"Do you want me to drop you off home?" I asked Sophie on the way back.

"No, thank you," she said. "I told Martin I would make paella tonight. As a thank you. I bought the ingredients in town. See?" She held up a bag of groceries.

The villa was empty when we returned. "Put those bags in your rooms, girls," I shouted as they dumped their stuff in the kitchen and disappeared outside. I left Sophie chopping onions and went to see where Jacob was. He was lying on a sunbed, wearing headphones and little else.

"Hi. Where's Dad?" I yelled.

"Gone for a walk with Ken and Linda." He yelled back. "Am I brown yet?"

"No, but you are pink." More attempts to impress Sophie, no doubt. "Maybe you ought to cover – "

An almighty crash made us both shoot round. Tilly and Mandy were standing either side of an upturned table. Mandy was in tears and Tilly was laughing like a demon.

"What the hell is going on?" I demanded.

"She threw my phone in the pool!" Mandy shrieked.

"Well, she stole my skull earrings!"

"Did not!"

"Did so!"

Sophie and Alice emerged from the kitchen. Jacob wandered over. And I stood my ground. "Tilly, apologise to Mandy. Mandy, give Tilly back her earrings. Jacob put a shirt on. And Sophie, get in the car. I'm taking you home."

I'd expected the girls to defend Sophie's departure. But I guess even they'd realised she'd finally outstayed her welcome.

***

"I can walk from here," she said as we pulled off the main road into a rather shabby area of town.

"You sure? Everything is uphill from here and it's sweltering out there."

Sophie shrugged so I drove on, looking for a good place to pull in.

"Stop the car," she shouted.

"I can't stop on a narrow – "

"Stop the car!"

"Okay," I said, pulling into the verge and switching off the engine. "But don't blame me if – " I was silenced by the look on Sophie's face. "You okay?"

I followed her eyes to a derelict farmhouse up ahead. The yard was cluttered with tin barrels, old tyres and rusty car parts. A large man in a dirty white vest was slumped outside on a broken chair. A bottle of beer spilled from his hand. Several empties lay at his feet. The man caught sight of us and began shouting obscenities. He staggered towards the car, screaming, "La puta! La perra!" Sophie drew back like a startled kitten.

"I'm not leaving you here," I said, turning the ignition. "Where's your house?" I could barely hear her reply.

"We're here. Thank you." Sophie opened the car door. "Papa's bark is worse than his bite."

I pulled her back in. It all made sense now. The reluctance to go home. The insistence that she walk from the bottom of the hill. She'd welcomed the break from her father and had been ashamed to let me see how she lived.

Her shame was nothing compared to mine. I'd no idea what I was going to do with her at the end of our holiday. Linda and I would figure something out. But I sure as hell wasn't going to leave her with that monster.

I thrust the car into reverse and backed down the hill as fast as was safely possible, Sophie's father still running after us and cursing.

"Thinking about it," I said, when we were back on the main road, "it would be a shame to waste all those paella ingredients. Why don't we go back to the villa, and you show me how to cook it?"

The cocky young woman who'd intimidated me all week dissolved into a vulnerable little girl. "I'd like that very much," she said.

"I'd like that too," I replied.

Dark knight

He had never done anything like this before. He was in a stranger's flat. A stranger's bedroom. A stranger's arms. The stranger was standing behind him, her breath on his neck, her flesh probing his. He felt terrified and tantalised in equal measures.

They'd met a few hours earlier in a dark night club in a particularly dark part of the city.

He'd been at an old boys' night out. A catch up with mates from Uni. They'd hoped to rekindle the carefree pleasure of their youth. In reality, their middle-aged hearts weren't really into it. Several had left early to get up for important meetings, school runs, dog walking, early commutes. Others had been more honest and said they couldn't hack late nights anymore.

But he'd promised himself a reckless night out and wasn't about to give up that easily. He'd been working flat out for months; he'd finally managed to free himself from Roseanne, and he was determined to do something brave that night. So, when most of his mates had buggered off home, he'd gone to a nightclub called Hell with a guy he'd barely remembered, let alone liked.

Within minutes, the guy had disappeared with a dodgy looking group, so he'd bought himself a Jack Daniels and decided that if nothing happened by the time he'd finished it, he'd admit defeat and get a taxi home.

Downing the last of his drink without even catching the eye of a woman, he'd manoeuvred his way through the darkness to find the toilets. Coming back out, he'd tripped over a drunk, and fell into her arms. He'd apologised. She'd laughed. Then they'd danced, chatted, flirted, snogged in the back of the taxi, and now they were in her bedroom with less clothing and even less inhibition.

He liked her being behind him. He liked her hands making his middle-aged body feel alive again. But he wanted to see her, to see himself with her. He wanted to be able to fix the image in his mind so he could recall it later. He manoeuvred their twisted bodies towards the mirror and saw his delight gazing back at him.

There he was, savouring the moment before he'd turn and take her. He closed his eyes, felt her breath, revelled in her body against his buttocks.

He opened his eyes to watch the scene in the mirror. There he was in ecstasy. But where was she? She had no reflection.

It was only when he felt the tiny pin prick in his neck, he realised why.

First dance

Simon hated to admit it, but Nicky had a point. Unconventional though it was, it did make sense for Brian, Nicky's ex, to give her away at the wedding. She'd been married twice already so having her father do it was… ludicrous.

Simon had switched off the radio in the Ford Transit so he could concentrate on the diversion signs. But now all he could think about was his impending wedding. Why was he even getting married at his age anyway?

He'd wanted to tell Nicky he was feeling uncomfortable with Bob, her first husband and the father of at least one of her three children, being his best man. Wasn't having another previous husband involved in the proceedings stretching his generosity just a bit too far? But he'd learned that when Nicky made her mind up about something, there really wasn't much point in arguing. Besides, it wasn't as if there was anyone else he could ask.

A sudden sign saying "A259 closed" brought Simon back to the job in hand. He was already running late and if he had to go all the way around Newhaven, as the sign was clearly implying, he'd be hard pushed to get to Hastings before noon. There would be no Slush Puppie at the Pavilion Café this lunchtime.

Simon had been a Slush Puppie technician for 41 years. He'd started in 1974, just a few months after Ralph Peters brought the now famous 'ice crystal drink' to the UK. He'd never intended to stay 41 years but there'd never been a good enough reason to leave. He enjoyed driving up and down the country, visiting cafés and leisure centres, installing the freezers, delivering the mixes and being on call if the machines broke down. It made him feel like a sort of superhero when the children cheered as the blue drink machine whirred back into action.

Long days on the road, and a teenage shyness he never got over, meant he'd had few friends and even fewer girlfriends. He'd never been terribly comfortable in female company, and male company left him feeling rather inadequate – hence the lack of a best man. Hence the lack of a best anything.

The diversion signs brought him onto the familiar A26, so he switched the radio back on, hoping to catch the end of Ken Bruce's 'Pop master'. Halfway through the second contestant's round, the programme switched itself off and his phone rang. He'd only recently been introduced to the joys of Bluetooth, and it still surprised him when Nicky's voice came out of his radio.

"We... come... dance."

"I'm sorry, sweetheart, I lost most of that."

"D.. ay ... firs... ance..."

"First glance?"

"Dance! Dance!"

He managed to say he was going to pull

over and call her back before the line went dead. He drove on until he was clear of the hills and pulled into a layby.

From what he could gather, Nicky had been talking to the DJ – she'd also been talking to the florist, the dress maker, the hairdresser and her 'ungrateful' daughter – and he, the DJ, had asked what song they'd like for their first dance. They didn't need to decide right away, but could they let him know by the end of the week because it might take him a bit of time to track it down. He'd supposed that since neither of them were "spring chickens" they might want something a bit obscure.

The DJ had been kind enough, Nicky explained, to offer a list of popular first dance songs in case they were struggling to find something. These included 'Lady in Red' by Chris de Burgh, 'Wonderful Tonight', by Eric Clapton and 'The Wonder of You' by Elvis. Nicky had been a little put out by the last suggestion and said, "How old does he think we are?" Ancient, had been Simon's silent answer, but mentioning age to Nicky was another thing he'd learned not to do.

The conversation had ended with Nicky telling Simon she couldn't even remember what songs she'd had for her previous two weddings, and he should "have a think about it" and call her back. In the meantime, she'd have a word with Brian since he was the "musical one in the family".

While Simon had become accustomed to many things with Nicky, he'd never quite got used to the inclusion of both of her ex-husbands in every family event.

Back in his van, Hastings still at least an hour away, he couldn't help wondering, and not for the first time, if he was doing the right thing in marrying Nicky. Surely the fact they didn't even have a special song was a sign.

He'd met Nicky when she'd worked in 'The Cod Father' in Southampton. The Slush Puppie machine had been installed in the fish and chip shop on a trial basis but after six weeks and five call-outs, the owner had told Simon where to stuff it.

As Simon was loading the machine back into his van, Nicky had confessed she'd sabotaged it on purpose to see Simon again. He'd been enormously flattered – and slightly bewildered – by her actions and when she suggested he come round to her place for dinner one night, he hadn't had the heart to refuse. Six months later, she (and her three grown up children) had moved into his small but comfortable semi. Now, they were two weeks off getting married.

Lost in the image of his uncertain future, it took Simon a moment or two to recognise the song on the radio. At first, he thought it was 'Can't Help Falling In Love' but then he realised it was 'Plaisir D'amour', the original French song on which the Elvis song was based.

There had been umpteen recordings of 'Plaisir D'amour' over the years, but this was HIS 'Plaisir D'amour', the 1965 Marianne Faithful version that had been playing THAT summer when his mother had taken in a French student for the first and – as it turned out – last time.

It was 1972. Simon was 15 and feeling rather anxious at the prospect of having a French boy staying in his room for a week. However, any anxiety he'd been feeling was nothing compared to how he felt when his mother opened the front door to Jeanne, a frighteningly pretty 14-year-old French girl.

After a brief phone call to check if the girl was in the right place, he and his mother realised that 'Jeanne' was not an unusual spelling of 'Jean'.

Both too polite and embarrassed to admit their mistake, neither said anything to Jeanne, the school or each other. His mother had simply made the girl a cup of tea then dashed upstairs to remove the continental quilt and put-me-up from Simon's room and throw them into what had been affectionately called 'the music room' – a large cupboard that housed his father's old 78 rpm record collection.

It had been the most miserable and most exhilarating week of Simon's life. The 'music room' was barely five-foot-long and the put-me-up took on a new level of discomfort when not fully extended. His mother had attempted to cook French food to make the girl feel "at home", despite Simon suggesting that one of things the students wanted to experience was English home cooking. But the biggest disappointment of the week was Jeanne's total lack of interest in him: she barely said a dozen words a day to him. She chose instead to meet up with her fellow French students at every opportunity.

There was, however, one English boy the French girls did choose to spend time with – John Sutherland. Just a few months' shy of his sixteenth birthday, John Sutherland towered above every boy in the school – and most of the teachers. He was impossibly good looking, a natural at sports and genuinely funny. Of all John's attributes, humour was the one Simon envied most.

On the positive side, Jeanne spent most of the week in tiny vests and shorts and, on the rare occasions when she did talk to Simon, she called him "See-mon", pursing her lips slowly on the long, sensuous 'mon'.

It was the Friday evening, the night before the students went home, and the school was hosting a discotheque. Simon had fought with himself all day. His rational side knew he'd hate it. The other boys would ridicule him, Jeanne would ignore him, and his mother would make him wear proper trousers and a tie. But the wishful side, the side that realised Jeanne was going home tomorrow and he'd never see her again, wouldn't be silenced. Even watching her dancing with John Sutherland was better than staying home and watching "Sale of the Century".

Decision made, the evening began to go in his favour. He somehow managed to get out the house without his mum noticing he was wearing jeans and a t-shirt, the other boys seemed as nervous as he was, and Jeanne was being strangely friendly towards him. At least she was every time John Sutherland walked past with his arm draped across the shoulders of Anne-Marie, a tiny French girl with disproportionately large breasts.

There had been a few hopeful moments when it appeared as if Jeanne wanted to dance with him, but it wasn't until the headmaster, Mr Ritchie, announced he had "something rather special for our French cousins" that the moment came. There had been a few groans when Marianne Faithful's 'Plaisir D'amour' first crackled out of the speakers (and a few rebellious shouts of "we want Slade") but as the hormone-ridden teenagers began to sway to the French music, the complaints petered out.

Simon had been transfixed by John Sutherland and his 'way with the girls'. They seemed to find everything he said hilariously funny, and now, as John Sutherland's torso pressed up against Anne-Marie's breasts, Simon's admiration rose to a new level.

Suddenly, he felt Jeanne's breath on the side of his face. "See-mon," she said, pursing her lips beautifully. "Dance with me."

Jeanne pulled Simon onto the dance floor, manoeuvring them closer to her rival, watching intently as the tall boy bent his head to kiss Anne-Marie's tiny, upturned face. Simon knew exactly what he was, how Jeanne was using him. But, no matter, because every time she turned to relocate the necking pair, her pert little breasts brushed against his bare arm, sending shivers of 'Plaisir d'amour' down his spine and beyond.

Jeanne departed early the next morning, leaving a scribbled note on the kitchen table thanking them for a "most pleasant week" and promising "See-mon" an enormous hug and kiss if he were ever in Lyon.

The pips blasted out of the radio and Simon realised he'd missed the Hastings turn off. He sighed, pulled over and called the manager of the Pavilion Café.

Two weeks later, after Brian had 'given' Nicky to Simon, and Bob had delivered the best man's speech, the DJ's voice rang out over the PA system.

"Could I have your attention please, ladies and gentlemen? The bride and groom will shortly be taking to the floor for the first dance."

There was a flurry of activity as people gathered around the newlyweds. Bob, Brian and three assorted offspring grinned over at Simon and Nicky expectantly. Simon felt an odd sensation in his stomach and an even odder one in his chest. Nicky grabbed Simon's arm and pulled him onto the dance floor.

She was already singing the first few lines of "Everything I do" by Bryan Adams when Marianne Faithful's voice gently filled the room.

"What the heck is that?" Nicky snapped. "I'll kill that flaming DJ!"

"I chose it," said Simon, more masterfully than he felt. He pulled Nicky's ample middle into his and pressed his hand on her bottom.

He had heard about women melting into a man's arms, but he'd never actually experienced it. Until now. As his wife succumbed to his touch, he leant forward and whispered in her ear, "Call me See-mon".

And she did.

Getting on with Freya

"It's not healthy, Freya." Clare waved her glass of Cabernet Sauvignon inches from my face. Her bossiness reached new levels when she'd been drinking. "That sort of relationship with an ex-husband is not healthy."

I sometimes wondered why I remained friends with Clare. We'd met almost 20 years ago during a youth theatre production of 'Grease', and I'd fallen in love with her instantly. She was everything I wasn't. Tall, slim, elegant with an abundance of dark curls and a smile that made you do stupid things. Everyone adored her, and if you hung around long enough some of that adoration rubbed off on you.

"Do you want another drink?" I asked. It wasn't my round, but I needed time to think.

"I shouldn't," she said, reapplying her already impeccably applied lipstick. "But if you're insisting."

The remainder of the evening passed without further talk of my 'unhealthy relationship'. Clare seemed much happier droning on about Tommy re-redecorating the spare room (the mocha feature wall was too dark), Sasha hating the orthodontist (the 'Invisalign Alignment System' wasn't actually invisible) and her new BMW 3 Series M Sport not being delivered until June.

"You are coming to my birthday party on Saturday, aren't you?" Clare said, getting out of the taxi. It didn't seem appropriate to remind her I was helping Graham move into his new flat, so I muttered a feeble "course I am" as she disappeared indoors.

As the taxi pulled away, I could see the driver in the mirror smirking. I asked him what was so funny.

"Sorry," he said, glancing round at me. "She's your buddy. I should keep my opinions to myself."

"Yes, you should," I said, aware I sounded a bit too Maggie Smith. "But you've got me curious now."

It was delightful listening to a man (and a pretty cute one at that) telling me how lovely I seemed and what a right pain in the arse my friend was. By the time we'd got to my front door, I'd established that his name was Nick, he was 32, from Manhattan, currently single, doing a master's in creative writing, and keen to go for drink with me sometime. I was flattered, uncomfortable and convinced he was winding me up. But I took his card, insisted on paying the fare and walked in my door with a big grin on my face.

The grin dropped immediately when I realised that my house phone was ringing. I almost never answered the landline, knowing it to be either a sales call or my mother. But it was almost midnight, and not even the PPI callers were that vigilant.

"Ah. You're still awake. Good." It was

Graham, confident as always that I was as keen to talk to him as he to me. "It's about Saturday. I need you to do a few things for me."

I'd agreed to help him move because his car was playing up and, according to Graham, I "sort of owed it to him" since it was, technically, still my flat too. It wasn't. I'd relinquished my share as part of the divorce settlement, but there didn't seem much point arguing.

"Can you bring cleaning stuff?" He made the words 'cleaning stuff' sound as if it was illegal drugs. "Oh, and the hoover has packed in, so you'll need to bring yours." He continued to list various chores we needed to do on Saturday, and I was just on the verge of suggesting he might like to do a few of them beforehand when he did that thing he always did. He turned the conversation round to me.

"So, how have you been, Babe? Still working too hard?" And that was it. We were back on our favourite subject, and I was well and truly reeled in. Again.

It was nearly one by the time I'd got to bed but I'd enjoyed talking to Graham and was no longer feeling quite so abused. The following morning, I wished I'd gone to bed earlier.

By Friday night, I still hadn't summoned the courage to tell Clare I wasn't likely to make it to her party. Of course, if she'd been holding it in the evening, like normal 36-year-olds, it wouldn't be a problem. But since Clare had become a mother, all our lives centred round her kids. She no doubt wanted to wheel them out in their latest designer braces to show the world what a success she and Tommy had made of life.

I finished my Chinese, switched off the TV and rang Clare. Tommy answered. "Hello Freya. It's lovely to hear your voice." He sounded tired. Tommy always sounded tired. "Are you looking forward to tomorrow?" For a moment, I wondered how he knew Graham was moving.

"I can't make the party, I'm afraid. That's what I'm phoning about."

"Oh," said Tommy. "Then let me put you onto Clare." I was very tempted to hang up, but she'd only ring back and be in an even worse mood, so I hung on. Obligingly.

"What's this about you not coming to my party?" Clare asked in her 'but I'll be miserable without you' voice. It was a trick I pretty much always fell for.

"I can't... I'm helping Graham move into his flat and I won't be back in time." My voice was shaky but more with excitement than nerves.

"Oh, for pity's sake, Freya. When will you see what that man is doing to you?" Clare carried on for several minutes. I'd heard it all before.

What was the point in leaving him two years ago if all I was going to do was run every time he clicked his fingers? Why couldn't I see how he was manipulating me? When was I going to admit that I was still in love with him?

I let her run out of steam. She did eventually. Then I said, "goodbye Clare, thank you for your advice" and hung up.

The feeling of empowerment lasted about 10 minutes. I spent the next hour justifying my decision and by the time the 10 o'clock news had started I'd called her back, said I'd get away from Graham's as quickly as possible and wouldn't miss her birthday party for the world.

Lying in bed later, I kept playing snatches of conversations in my head. But no matter how hard I tried, Clare and Graham retained the upper hand. Even in my make-believe conversations, I lost the argument! I clearly fell asleep at some point because the next thing I knew I was dreaming the school bell was ringing. Only it wasn't the school bell, it was my phone and Graham's name was emblazoned on the screen.

"Are you okay, Babe?" He sounded genuinely concerned.

"Er...I think so... shouldn't I be?"

"I thought you'd have been here by now. I was worried you'd had an accident."

I'd forgotten to set my alarm, which meant I'd be late getting there, late getting away and late getting to Clare's party. I threw on some jeans and a t-shirt, grabbed the vacuum cleaner, the entire contents of the utility cupboard and a packet of ready salted crisps for breakfast.

The first thing that struck me when I got to

Graham's was how little he'd done. "Couldn't you have started yourself?" I ventured to ask.

"Oh, you know what I'm like, Babe. You do packing so much better than me. Want a coffee?"

The second thing that struck me was a woman. A very young, skinny and sort of attractive (if you went for that urchin look) woman in ripped jeans and a tatty vest.

"Oh. Hello." I forced the biggest grin ever onto my face. "I don't think we've met. I'm Freya. Graham's ex. Ex-wife. We're divorced."

"Yeah, of course," Graham said. "You don't know Tanya, do you? Tanya, this is Freya, my…"

"Ex-wife. I hear," said the impossibly young Tanya.

"Freya, this is Tanya. She's from Bulgaria. Do you want some coffee too, Babe?" I was momentarily confused by the reference to Babe since he'd already offered me coffee.

"No," Babe 2 answered. "I not drink caffeine today."

I not do much at all today, I couldn't help thinking, but chose to simply look at her with as much disdain as she looked at me.

"What's first?" Graham asked, reaching over me to get a couple of mugs from the cupboard. His chest pushed against his shirt, making me feel uncomfortable.

I moved away and unpacked various cloths and bottles from the bags I'd brought with me.

"You like egg?" It took me a second to realise that Babe 2 was talking to me. "I make egg. You like some?"

"No. Thank you. I've come here to work. To help Graham leave what was our marital home and move into his new pad that I'm pretty much funding." I didn't actually say the last bit. But I wanted to. Oh, did I want to.

After I'd wrapped our old mugs and plates in tissue paper, vacuumed the bedroom we'd once shared, took down curtains I'd hung 10 years ago and cleaned the bath Babe 2 had probably used an hour earlier, Graham thanked me for being "such a star" and asked me what I thought of Tanya. I was tired, angry and in no mood for pleasing.

"I'm not getting into this." I wiped dust off the curtains and placed them in a box.

"What does that mean?" Graham threw some sheets and towels into a holdall.

"You don't really want to know what I think of her; you just want to tell me what you think of her. And I don't want to know."

"You don't like her, do you?"

"I am not having this conversation." I looked round for my plastic gloves and headed back to the bathroom. Graham followed me.

"She's older than she looks. She's 24. And

bright. Fiercely bright. Speaks seven languages. Seven!"

I turned on him sharply. "Why are you doing this? Why are you asking me what I think of some girl in your kitchen that I've never seen before and have no interest in? What am I even doing here? Yes, what in God's name am I actually doing here?"

I ripped off my Marigolds, threw them at him and stormed out. Or at least I tried to, but I got wedged between the vacuum cleaner and the top of the stairs and, in trying to free myself, I knocked over a large pile of vinyls Graham had inherited from his dad. I watched them slipping out of their covers and sliding down the stairs – The Beatles, The Who, The Rolling Stones, David Bowie, Pink Floyd – old stuff we'd listened to in our early years when we pretended we weren't into Oasis, Blur and Radiohead.

Lack of sleep, lack of breakfast and two years of guilt-ridden niceties rose to the surface, and I burst, unceremoniously, into tears. "It's okay, Babe," Graham said, putting his big arms around my waist. "They're more resilient than CDs. They'll be fine."

"I don't give a shit about your stupid vinyls, you idiot! And I don't give a shit about your stupid Bulgarian girlfriend!" It wasn't one of history's best put-downs, but it fired me up and the next diatribe was far more effective. "Ten years, ten years I put up with your ridiculous notions of fame and fortune. Ten years of listening to your talentless music, your self-obsessed equally pathetic talentless friends. Of supporting you financially, emotionally and physically! Ten years!"

Graham looked genuinely shocked. He even had the sense to wave Tanya away when she dragged herself out of the kitchen to see what all the shouting was about.

"And do you know what pisses me off most? Do you?" I waited for Graham to speak. He didn't. "That! That total inability to say or do anything! Do you know your only response to every problem? Do you?" He clearly didn't. *"What would you like me to do?* What would you like me to do! I'll tell you what I would have liked you to do, Graham. I would have liked you to have thought-through your problems yourself. I would have liked you to have been the man for once and taken some responsibility for your actions. I would have liked you to have taken care of me!"

I was aware that I was now screaming but there was nothing I could do to stop the outpouring. What was more, I wasn't just ranting about Graham. I had suddenly dragged Clare into the conversation.

"I wanted to go to Durham university. But Clare sulked and said she couldn't bear for me to be so far away while she was expecting. So, I went to Reading instead. I wanted a white wedding in a church. But you wanted to get married on holiday. So, we married in Greece. Clare wanted me to be Sasha's godmother. But I said I felt uncomfortable taking vows when I wasn't religious. I became Sasha's godmother. I wanted to buy that cottage with the south-facing vegetable plot. But you wanted somewhere just off the high street with a recording studio in the basement. So, we bought this place. I hated this place. I hated Clare and I hated you. Except I didn't, I loved you. I still love you and that makes me hate you even more!"

I dodged the vinyls, grabbed my bag and ran outside. I could hear Graham calling my name. But he didn't exactly chase after me. And I could see Tanya's silhouette in the doorway as I drove away.

I'd cried so many times since I'd left Graham, I didn't think it was possible to cry anymore. But it was. I cried so much I had to pull into a layby to calm myself. And then, I just stopped. I sort of caught my breath a few times, blew my nose, adjusted the mirror to see how dreadful I looked, then sighed audibly. There were no more tears.

Clare, for all her selfish demands, had been right about one thing. My relationship with my ex was unhealthy. Why it had taken me two years to realise it, I wasn't sure. But now that I had, I felt an overwhelming sense of relief. Complete and utter bliss.

I drove back to my flat, showered, dressed, warmed up some soup and called Clare. Both her mobile and landline went to voicemail. "Hi Clare. It's me. I'm home but I'm not coming to your party. I'll call you next week to explain. Or not. Bye."

Then I went to my purse and took out Nick's card.

"Nick de Souza. Your local cab. Your local hero. There for you 24/7."

It would be nice to have someone "there for me" I thought, but not today. Today, I was going to spend time with someone I'd been neglecting for 20 years, someone I'd overlooked and underestimated. Someone I was going to take care of in future.

"Freya," I said to my reflection. "Meet Freya. I think you two are going to get along just great." Then I went into the living room, put on 'Don't Look Back In Anger', and didn't.

I got life

I am looking into the face of my dead son.

It's a little chubbier than I remember it. The nose, a little wider; the cheeks, a little higher. The perfect lips that once suckled at my breast now stretch across a set of teeth too big for their delicate form.

But it is, without doubt, his face. Jack's face. My face. I reach out to touch it and it jerks away instinctively. I see fear in its eyes. Its dark, olive eyes, flecked with green and brown and amber. They are not Jack's eyes and my heart rages in agony.

"What did you say this was again?" Cameron wished the music in the van was as rhythmical as the windscreen wipers.

"Miles Davis," Bob answered. "*Kind of Blue.*" Bob spoke with an air of incredulity. Cameron was already regretting the question. "Only the finest studio album ever produced. Recorded in 1959 at Columbia's 30th Street Studio in New – "

"New York. Yeah. I remember. You told me earlier. I only wanted to know what song it was."

"Track."

Track. Song. Same thing, Cameron thought as Bob sucked in his breath. Clearly not the same thing. "You want me to take over the driving for a while?"

"This *track*," Bob pointed out, "is the only one on the album that features Wynton Kelly on piano. Davis's usual sextet consisted of Bill Evans on piano, Paul Chambers on bass and, of course, none other than John Coltrane on tenor sax…"

Cameron returned to the sound of the windscreen wipers as Bob whittered on about *Kind of Blue.* It was, Bob pointed out, regarded by many as the most influential album of its time, which was why it was ranked number 12 in the greatest blah blah…

Cameron wanted to ask Bob how he felt about Frank Lampard being sacked from Chelsea. But he suspected Bob would find a way of bringing the conversation back to Freddie Freeloader. If you love this album so much, Cameron thought, why do you talk all the way through it?

They'd been on the road the best part of four hours and Cameron was dying for a piss. But 'Whispering Bob Harris' was refusing to stop until they reached Southwaite, the last service on the M6. Their precious cargo contained a particularly special load tonight and they needed to get to Glasgow by 8.00am at the latest.

"Where did you do your IHCD training?" Bob asked.

"My what?"

"Your driver training? Where, at which site, did you do it?"

Grateful for something other than jazz filling

the 800 mile return journey, Cameron launched into a blow by blow account of his 7-day driver training at the North Weald Aerodrome in Essex. By the end, he'd bored himself and was actually grateful when Bob interrupted him with a raised finger and instructions to listen to the Coltrane solo on *All Blues*.

"I like Nina Simone," Cameron offered. But Bob's withered expression said more than words. And Cameron continued to feign interest for the next 38.5 miles. Never had a pee felt that good.

My son's face registers my pain. Its foreign eyes brim with tears and its once perfect lips quiver as they form the words "I'm sorry".

My hand reaches up to touch the all too familiar cheek, then stops, suspended, motionless, helpless.

Comfort break over and fuel tank full again, Bob took control of the passenger seat and the Sat Nav. "There appears to be some congestion on the M8," he advised, "but we're making good time and our ETA of eight hundred hours is more than feasible."

If Cameron had expected to listen to his choice of music during his driving stretch, he was sadly mistaken. After finally finding one radio station that played the occasional Bruce Springsteen or Guns & Roses number, the pathetic signal eventually lost all connection around Penrith.

"You never get a signal here," Bob explained. "Too many hills and valleys." He then ejected *Kind of Blue* from the CD player – and replaced it with *Bird Is Free* by Charlie Parker.

Maybe the foreman will put me on another job when we reach Glasgow, thought Cameron, and I'll be spared Johnny Dankworth on the journey home.

"Ever had to use your blue light training?" Bob asked. "You've haven't been with the firm long. I wondered if you've had a chance to go into full IHCD mode."

Before Cameron had the chance to explain this was in fact his first delivery, Bob was off on another monologue about 'modal soloing'.

"So why are we going all the way to Glasgow?" Cameron ventured to ask. "Surely they've got all this stuff up there, too."

"Not this load. We've got a WN347B12 in the back there. And you know what that means, don't you?"

Cameron sure as hell did. What was the chance he'd be delivering a WN347B12 on his first sortie? What was the chance he'd be delivering a WN347B12 ever!

Suddenly, travelling with jazz wasn't quite so bad after all. He felt both excited and terrified. Who was it for? Who was it from? What was happening in Glasgow right now? Somebody somewhere was relying on him to deliver a WN347B12!

There's another face next to my son's. A woman's face with the same hazel and amber eyes. Older eyes, but unmistakably the same.

Despite the tears that flow from them, these are smiling eyes. As is her mouth. I watch it move deliberately, forming shapes. The lips part and the tongue is placed between the top and bottom teeth. A sound is emitted. The lips pout and I read the words. "Thank you. Thank you. How can we ever begin to thank you?"

They were just 24 miles from Glasgow and making good time when the traffic heading north on the M74 came to a halt. Squinting into the distance, Cameron figured the line of stationary traffic stretched a good few miles ahead of them.

"No problem," Bob said, picking up the two-way radio. "I'll call base and let them know we're rerouting. Put the light on and make your way over to the hard shoulder – easy – and undertake until we reach junction 5."

The traffic seemed to part like the Red Sea as Cameron pulled over. Thank God they hadn't turned the M74 into a Smart Motorway! As instructed by Bob, he drove at a steady 25mph: 35mph slower than they needed to get to their destination by 8.00am.

"Shit," Cameron said as they approached the Old Carlisle Road. "Everyone's had the same idea." The clock on the dash showed 7.23. They had 37 minutes to do a 40-50 minute journey. "Do you want to take the wheel?"

"Navigating is a harder than driving," Bob answered. "Especially when you have to keep one eye on the road, one eye on the Sat Nav, and another on the WN347B12."

Cameron nodded. He had a feeling he was going to agree with whatever Bob said or did from now on.

"You look so much like him," I say to the young man that now occupies my son's face. Or rather, I try to say it.

My words battle through three sets of tears. Is this really happening? It's a dream, surely. A nightmare. I'll wake up now. Jack will wake me.

Bob punched the CD out of the player and zoomed in on the Sat Nav screen. "Okay," he barked. "Proceed 600 yards north-east on the B7086 and turn left at Knoweknack Terrace. 300 yards. 200. Slower! You almost knocked that kid off his bike. What gear are you in?"

Cameron's palms were so wet, he could barely hold the wheel. The shrill of the siren was making him so tense, cramp had set in on his left foot, and his right knee throbbed.

"At the roundabout, take the 1st exit and stay on the B7078," Bob said. "Good. Okay, take the next left. Left! And watch out for – What is it with these people? Right, keep in – Where are you going? You can't go – "

"You said 'right'!"

"I meant – Okay, you're going straight on at

the traffic lights and – damn. There's a dust cart in the middle of the – okay, pull into the path – "

"The path? You sure?"

"Careful! Dog walkers!"

Jack will tell me he's running late so he's going to take his bike. I'll try to protest. But he'll put a finger to mouth and tell me to trust him. And I will. As I always did.

The clock on the dash read 7.52. Cameron wanted to ask how far they were from Gartnavel hospital but was terrified of the answer. The A82 was moving, but not as fast as Cameron hoped. Bob called base again. The prognosis wasn't looking good. The team had hoped the delivery would have been made by now. 8.00am was the absolute latest.

"You're doing great," Bob said, much to Cameron's surprise. "But there's roadworks up ahead so we're going to come off at Shelley Road. It's going to be busy. Commuters. School runs...You can do it."

Bob's voice became Cameron's spinal cord. He no longer thought for himself. He allowed Bob to conduct his actions like a jazz *tour de force*. "Left. Right. Change up. Change down. Swerve. Wait. Accelerate. Pull back. Foot down. Right. Left. Change up. Change up. Good. Foot down. Faster. Faster. Right. Left. Slow. Slow. Stop!"

They were there waiting. Two clinicians: one holding a cryogenic container, the other a mobile. Bob shot out of the cab and dropped the

WN347B12 into the container. They both shouted thank you as they ran into the hospital.

"Cup of tea and a bacon sandwich?" Bob said as he stepped back into the ambulance. Cameron wept. Bob smiled and picked up the *Nuff Said* CD. "How about something cheerier, eh?" Nina Simone's *I Got Life* filled the cab.

My Jack had not died in vain. The head injury that brutally cut short his young life had left his kidneys, liver, heart and face intact. Four people had been given another chance of life. And this 19 year old boy, whose face had been ripped off when his long hair caught in a threshing machine, can now eat without straws and go out without shame.

Slowly, so very, very slowly, the pain in my heart lessens. Seeing my dead son's face alive and animated, holding a mother who has also experienced tragedy, fills me with a gratitude I hadn't believed was possible. Together, we bless every one of the 286 surgeons, doctors, nurses, clinicians, therapists, researchers, cleaners and blue light drivers who, one year ago today, made it all possible.

The Legend of Jonny Spry

Sunday. 11.58. Heathrow Terminal 3. A man saunters wearily along the endless corridors to Arrivals. He watches groups of people speed past him. Everyone eager to escape 'No Man's Land' and embark on the next leg of life's journey.

He enters Arrivals, sighs, and looks at a long line of people holding up paper signs bearing names and company logos. He reads 'Keishin Hoshiro', 'Barbara Van Praag', 'Matt Abrahart', 'Mr J O'Brien' and stops at 'Jonny Spry'.

"Jonny Spry", he says to himself. "Nice."

He walks over to a tall, angular woman whose smile is more business-like than friendly. He likes that. "Jonny Spry," he says, offering his hand.

"Carrie Buckingham," she says. Her voice is crisp, assured. Her handshake, short and firm. "So glad to meet you at last. How was the flight?"

He remembers the size and smell of his fellow passengers and instinctively stretches. "A little cramped. You know how it is."

"Cramped? In first class?" Carrie Buckingham asks. "You do surprise me."

He senses his first slip-up but decides to brave it out. He smiles, shrugs and implies he's used to the better things in life.

"Well, I'm afraid you won't be able to stretch out quite yet." Carrie folds the Jonny Spry sign in half and places it in her large tote bag. "My driver has had to go elsewhere. So, we'll have a drink here, finalise a few details and then, when he returns, we'll drop you off at your hotel. Okay with you?"

"Sounds marvellous," he says, grinning with boyish excitement.

He follows her to Starbucks. Or Costa. Or Pret. They all look the same to him. They sit at a table too small for two and Carrie removes her coat. She places it neatly over the back of her chair and suggest two flat whites. He agrees wholeheartedly.

As she walks to the counter, he quickly rips the labels off his case and stuffs them into the zip compartment at the front. He then picks up her coat, inhales the perfume and feels inside the pockets. He removes a lipstick from one, a handkerchief from the other then replaces them and the coat with seconds to spare. Starbucks service has clearly improved.

She places two paper cups on the table and sits down.

"Thank you," he says. "Cheers!"

"Oh, I think we can do better than that." Carrie seems to have lightened up. "What do they say in your country?"

"Er… have a nice day?"

"In Mexico? Really?"

"Ha!" Second slip-up. He thinks quickly.

"That's globalisation for you. We're all just one big Ronald McDonald these days."

"Indeed, we are." Her mobile rings. She checks the caller ID. "I'm sorry. I need to take this." She answers. "Speak... No... Not now... This evening... Goodbye." She places her phone on the table. "So, Jonny... I can call you Jonny, can't I?"

"Why not?" He laughs.

"And you must call me Carrie."

"Well, it's nice to meet you... properly... at last." He seems to have got away with it.

"How do you feel about Tuesday?" she asks.

"It's my second favourite day of the week."

"Does that give you enough time?" She either doesn't get his humour or is choosing to ignore it.

"This Tuesday?"

"This Tuesday. The 6th. Yes. Is that a problem for you?"

"No. Tuesday's fine." He takes a sip of coffee. It tastes of re-boiled water and charcoal.

Carrie asks if he has everything he needs and indicates his suitcase. He nods. It seems to be expected of him. "But if not," she says, "talk to Rogers. You are seeing Rogers later, aren't you?"

"Rogers? Yes... later."

"You don't seem very certain. You're not trying to hide anything from me, are you Mr Spry?"

"What happened to 'Jonny'?"

"You tell me."

"Sorry," he says, thinking on his feet. "Jet lag. I still think it's Wednesday." Carrie softens. A little.

"So, tell me, Mr Spry – "

"I liked it best when you called me Jonny."

Carrie leans forward and lowers her voice. "Mr Spry. I am not prepared to pay you five million pounds to be treated like a fool."

"Quite right. I'd treat you like a fool for a lot less."

"Now look – " Her phone rings again. She answers the call and speaks as monosyllabically as before. He watches as her expression changes from mild irritation to controlled rage. "I see. Yes. Thank you."

She hangs up, puts the phone back in her bag and pulls out what looks like a 9mm pistol hidden under a Hermes silk scarf. She points the concealed gun at him. "Make one false move and I'll blow your brains out."

He laughs. "Make one false move and I'll blow your brains out? It's a bit cliched, isn't it?"

"Who Are You?" she demands.

"Jonny Spry?"

"Jonny Spry is dead."

"You sure?"

"That was Helsinki on the phone. Jonny Spry was murdered in Mexico two days ago. You had better stop fucking with me and start talking!"

"Better," he says. "Definitely sounding more threatening now." He's enjoying himself far more than he thought possible.

Carrie's voice drops several tones. "I'll give you precisely 10 seconds to start talking and if you don't, I will call security and have you arrested!"

"For what?" he asks, remaining remarkably calm. "You're the one making out you have a gun under – " She looks down at the shape beneath her scarf. "You're the one planning some underhand job. I'm just some guy who got off a plane from Amsterdam and walked over to a woman holding up a sign."

Carrie opens her mouth, hesitates then closes it without saying a word. He watches as she computes the last ten minutes and figures it out. "You bastard! Who are you? Who are you working for?"

"I'm Bill. Bill Williams." He removes the scarf from her hand and reveals a small hairbrush. "Well, William Williams really but I changed it to Bill."

"Why?"

"Because William Williams sounds so…"

"Why did you pretend to be Jonny Spry, you idiot!"

"I liked the name," he says without a hint of irony. "It's a great name, isn't it?" He says it a few times, enjoying playing with the sound and movement. "Jonny Spry. Jonny Spry! He's... well he's the guy who meets beautiful women at airports... He's the guy who gets hired to do £5 million jobs..."

"He's the guy who gets murdered in Mexico."

"Good point, well made," he admits. "But, come on, haven't you ever looked at all those people in Arrivals and wondered what would happen if you walked up to one of them?"

He expects her to accuse him of being stupid, childish, inconsiderate and downright cruel. What he doesn't expect is tears. He can't handle tears.

She places the hairbrush back in her bag and uses the silk scarf to wipe away the tears, a glob of mascara and a rather unattractive amount of nasal secretion. He waits what he considers to be a polite amount of time then asks, conspiratorially, "Was he a hit man? Were you going to have someone knocked off?"

"Don't be ridiculous!" Carrie stuffs the scarf back in her bag. "He was an art dealer. I hired him to steal a painting so I could..." She stops herself. "What am I doing? You could be anyone. Who are you? Oh, God, you're not..."

"Do I look like a copper? Seriously?" Bill begins to feel a little bit guilty. "Tell me about the painting. I know a bit about art."

"I'm not really stealing it," she says, appearing grateful to have the chance to let it all out. "It's mine. Well, ours. But we need the money. I thought that if I could 'have it stolen', I could sell it on the black market AND claim the insurance money."

Bill is more fascinated than judgemental but something on his face gives Carrie the wrong impression.

"Don't look at me like that. Daddy's unwell. The ancestral home is falling to pieces. And I need at least £25 million to save it and the staff. Some of them have been with the family for generations. I can't throw them on the scrap heap now."

A sucker for the femme fatale, Bill hears himself saying "I'll do it." She is unimpressed and scoffs.

"Where did I say I flew in from?" he asks.

"Mexico."

"No. That was Jonny Spry."

"Amsterdam!"

"And what's Amsterdam famous for…?" He looks at her expectantly.

"Drugs? Sex? Canals?"

"Art!" Bill exclaims. "Dutch Masters! The Rijksmuseum! That's where I work. I can steal and sell your painting."

Carrie laughs and stands up. "I think you've wasted enough of my time."

"I'm the fake spotter," he says quickly.

"The what?"

"The best in the business. I can smell a fake at 15 feet." Carrie laughs and walks away. He raises his voice. "I have a condition known as hyperosmia – a highly acute sense of smell. Any good forger can recreate a masterpiece. But they can't recreate the original materials. The oils, the pigments, the canvasses, they all have their own distinctive scents."

Carrie continues to walk away. He calls after her. "Your perfume is Bulgari Jasmin Noir. You wash your hair with White Truffle Shampoo. Total waste of money." Carrie stops. "You have a Golden Retriever," he continues, "and you had your coat dry cleaned a week ago. Am I right?"

She turns and walks back. "Okay," she says. "You have my attention."

"So," he says, sitting back down. "Where's this painting you want me to steal?"

Loose change

Firefighter Sarah Christie was at the scene of the accident within 90 seconds of the crash.

Carnage was an overused word in her line of work. But it was how she'd later describe it at the inquest. A Ford transit lay flattened under an aircraft fuselage. A wedding car was bent in half. Fuel escaping from petrol tanks ignited a 50-foot fireball. And plumes of black smoke belted into the sky.

"How the hell did this happen?" Sarah Christie asked no-one in particular.

***

By British summer standards, it was surprisingly warm for two o'clock in the morning. Sauntering home from the casino, Edwardo Da Luz thanked the blackbirds for their song and tossed his lucky penny into the air.

He was feeling good. Really good. It had been a successful day at the races, and an even more successful night at the casino. To celebrate, he'd challenged a table of Chinese businessmen to a game of heads or tails. And won.

Watching the coin flip and return to his hand, Edwardo Da Luz considered the demise of cash. Few people used it these days. Fewer still had lucky pennies. But Edwardo liked cash. He liked touching it, counting it, piling it high and admiring the assorted towers. He thought digital currency was the best and worst thing that had happened to gambling: best for the online betting sites – worst for the punters.

"Damn," he said, as a momentary lapse of judgement sent his penny off in the wrong direction. He quickened his pace as it rolled ahead of him, building momentum, gathering speed and racing towards a roadside drain. "No-o-o-oh," he called as he watched the penny fall between the grating. A barely audible splash seemed to silence the birds.

***

Phyllis Harrison had a soft spot for sewage. Most people were ignorant of the marvels of waste and drainage. They had little respect for the complex infrastructure that made up the 68,000 miles of sewers in the Southeast – and even less for the gullies that protected the open metal gratings on roadsides.

She had been called out to inspect yet another damaged highway drain cover. Someone had clearly tried to retrieve a fallen key, mobile phone, wallet, purse, piece of jewellery or something else they valued more than public property.

Tree branches were usually the first tool – shortly followed by metal coat hangers, fishing rods, hammers, crowbars and even piledrivers. Clearly, the item this owner was determined to rescue last night must have been extremely precious. She'd never seen a gully cover quite so badly mangled.

Bending down awkwardly to get a better view of the damage, Phyllis Harrison let out a piercing yell. "Please," she begged to the gods. "Not the disc. Not the disc again!"

***

"I'm skating on thin ice," Ethan Carnegie said to himself as he read the note A&E had sent up with the woman.

Emily had gone to extreme lengths to remind him how important it was to leave work on time this evening. Her sister's engagement dinner was the last chance she'd give him to meet her family.

They'd been living together for the best part of a year and no excuse for his not attending tonight would be good enough this time.

It had already gone six when Dr Sharma sent the woman with crippling back pain up to the X-Ray department. She'd been in Accident and Emergency for nearly 10 hours and looked totally drained.

Ethan Carnegie adopted his most sympathetic voice. "I'm so sorry," he said. "My colleague is running late, and I need to leave now. Are you okay to wait a little longer... er..?" He looked again at her note. "Phyllis."

The woman didn't need to answer. It was obvious from her face and the almost animal sounding whine that emitted from her throat that she needed immediate diagnosis and treatment.

Ethan Carnegie smiled and led the woman into the X-Ray room.

***

Josie O'Hagan had heard more sob stories as a barmaid than Simon Bates ever did on Radio 1's long running Our Tune slot.

Funny how most of the stories came from men. Maybe women had more girlfriends they could moan to. She generally just nodded, made sympathetic noises and splashed a bit more beer into their pint glasses. But this guy tonight was piquing her interest.

If what he was saying was true, his girlfriend sounded like a right dickhead. If you could call a woman a dickhead. Chucking him out because he was late for a family dinner? That was a bit rough – especially as he'd stayed late at the hospital to see to some poor soul who'd fallen down a drain hole or something.

Maybe because he seemed like a decent bloke. Maybe because he looked a bit like Hugh Grant when he ran his hand through his floppy fringe. Maybe she just wanted to do something nice. But whatever it was, when it came to chucking out time Josie O'Hagan found herself offering him the use of her caravan for a day or two. Just until he could sort himself out.

The guy thanked her for her kindness, politely refused and asked for another whisky. "Honestly," Josie O'Hagan said, reluctant to pour him another drink. "You'd be doing me a favour.

We haven't had many bookings this summer and it could do with someone giving it a bit of an airing."

***

Katy Lamb was never happier than when she was holding a clipboard and pen. Depending on which figures one looked at, there were around 1,000 caravan fires a year in the UK and caravan fire insurance inspector Katy Lamb could almost tell the cause within 50 yards of the burnt-out unit. But there were procedures to go through, and Katy Lamb always went through them meticulously.

She didn't need to read the fire officer's report to learn what had happened. Experience told her it was a classic case of lone man and copious amounts of alcohol. He'd got back from the pub late, hadn't eaten all evening, lit the gas to make a bacon and/or fried egg sandwich, fallen asleep and woken up in the nick of time to get out of the van before the gas cannister exploded. Going through the debris cemented her theory.

Back in her car, Katy Lamb read the report and awarded herself a tiny smile. Everything was just as she'd ascertained – except for one small detail. She had found no trace of the fire safety equipment the owner claimed had been in the van at the time of the fire.

No smoke alarm. No fire blanket. No extinguisher. No pay out.

A photograph taken by the owner on an iPhone at 19.38 on 15 June – three weeks before the fire – clearly showed evidence of the fire safety equipment. Katy Lamb sighed. Her insurance experience also stretched to theft, and it was not unusual for such items to be stolen from vans at the beginning of the holiday season.

Sadly, for the owner, whether or not the items had been stolen three weeks, three days or even three hours before the fire, their absence at the time of the incident voided her claim.

Katy Lamb looked at her watch. She needed to get back to feed her rather anxious Saluki. She quickly finished the report and closed the file.

As she drove home, she pictured the caravan owner learning of the insurance company's findings and sighed again. "If only," she thought out loud, "I wasn't so damned honest."

***

Gunter Schmidt should have been in seventh heaven. He'd always loved the Saluki breed – and now he had one for himself.

Capable of running 42 miles an hour, the Saluki was almost as fast as the Greyhound. But its sleek, blonde coat and its athletic stance (not dissimilar to a small, short-haired Afghan hound – should such a dog exist) made the Saluki more distinguished looking than its rather scrawny, timid racing cousin.

He'd taken ownership of the dog a couple of weeks ago. Someone at work had mentioned that a friend of a friend knew someone who knew someone who had to get rid of her Saluki quickly.

Something about her losing her job because she signed off a fraudulent insurance claim and had to move back in with her mother who was allergic to dogs.

However, watching the dog now, her long front legs perched on the windowsill, her back legs performing an erratic dance, Gunter Schmidt was having serious misgivings.

Pining for her previous owner, the dog cried most of the evening and all of the night. She might have cried all day, too, but Gunter Schmidt was out at work from seven in the morning until six in the evening. Perhaps he should check with his neighbour.

***

Alan Edwards was a reasonable man. Beggars can't be choosers. Live and let live. Each to their own. Etc. But the constant whining from next door's new dog was driving him insane.

"I'm going to have to say something," he said to his wife over breakfast that morning. "I've been struggling to sleep all week and I barely slept at all last night."

His wife, who famously slept through the 1987 hurricane, dutifully responded with concerned grunts and some useful advice about earplugs and the Citizens Advice Bureau. But Alan Edwards' mind had drifted to more important matters.

Maybe he could pop round to his sister's for a couple of hours. He needed to get some sleep before the Shoreham air show that afternoon. Performing a complex loop the loop manoeuvre in a Hawker Hunter jet was dangerous enough. Doing so having had no decent sleep for weeks was potentially fatal.

***

Flames reached temperatures of near 2,000 degrees Fahrenheit and molten Hawker Hunter jet parts spewed into the air. Sarah Christie shouted to onlookers to keep back.

When the ambulances arrived moments later, a young paramedic raced towards her. "What the fuck happened here?" Arjun Kumar said to no-one in particular.

One carrot gold

Something is happening. The long days of intense cold and little activity are changing. My surroundings are softer, warmer, busier. My neighbours, more mobile. Small stones move around me. Tiny roots push and wind their way into the wet darkness below. Another spring is beginning. Another chance that she will find me is approaching.

I no longer remember how many winters have passed. Nine? Ten? More? But I have never given up hope. How can I? I am a wedding band. A symbol of eternity. A circle with no beginning and no end. I am endless and eternal, an expression of true love. I will return to her. There will be a way.

"There's no hurry, sweetheart," Will had said, that day in Hatton Garden, his voice betraying a growing impatience. "The wedding's still two weeks away." He laughed then, attempting to make light of his words.

The manager, Mr Hart, coughed quietly at that. "Choosing a wedding band," he said, "a piece of jewellery you will wear for the rest of your life, cannot be rushed."

Hannah resisted Will's suggestion to try the late 19th century Italian band with its ghastly crescent moons above a filigree of forget-me-nots and vines. Hideous.

Then Mr Hart offered an Art Deco cigar band, engraved with orange blossom and hearts. Hearts? Really? I had expected more of him.

But Hannah knew what she wanted. Her fingers traced the tray of decorated bands etched with symmetrical scrolls, passed rings laced with twisted threads of precious metals, and stopped at me. She picked me up and placed me gently onto the fourth finger or her left hand. "It's like the one my gran wore," she said. "Simple. Pretty. Smoothed through years of caring for a large family."

Mr Hart explained that I was an Edwardian, 18-carat, rose gold wedding band, assayed in Birmingham in 1907. In remarkably good condition, I was a bargain at just £300. Will hesitated momentarily. He'd expected to pay significantly more. But Hannah was certain. I was just what she was looking for. Mr Hart suggested having me adjusted. I was a little loose on Hannah's slim hand. But Hannah was worried I'd be damaged in the process. "Who knows?" Will said, tapping Hannah's tummy lightly. "You might put on a little weight soon, anyway."

I was placed in a navy box with an ivory satin lining and opened several times by the excited Hannah on the journey home. I then rested in Will's sock drawer until given to Harry, Will's best man, the day before the wedding. I'd heard frightening tales of what happened to wedding rings in the hands of the best man. But Harry was a sensible chap and I remained safe until placed on a velvet cloth at 2.25pm on Saturday 18th October 2008 and then on Hannah's finger 45 minutes later. In fact, I remained safe for the next six months, 14 days and 11 hours.

It was a Tuesday evening and Hannah had arrived back from work a little later than usual. Still a little loose on Hannah's finger, I was quickly removed and placed near the kitchen sink as she peeled potatoes for bangers and mash. As she picked up the third potato, Will called to ask if he could bring a colleague home with him. The colleague was over from Finland for a few days and Will didn't want him to spend the evening alone in a hotel bar. Always willing to please, Hannah agreed immediately, hung up then realised she needed to prepare something a bit more special than bangers and mash. From what I've heard about Finnish food, I would have thought bangers and mash *was* something special.

Anyhow, she frantically threw open the fridge, the larder and several cookery books before settling on 'curry in a hurry'. The 'hurry' aspect of the curry recipe did not seem to take into account the amount of time it took to chop onions, garlic, celery, carrots, courgettes and peppers.

Glancing at the clock as she fried the spices, Hannah panicked. Will and the Finnish colleague would be home in minutes and there wasn't one inch of free space on the worktops. I tried to glisten as much as I could as she grabbed a cloth and swept peelings, seeds, soggy bits and me into the compost bin.

I wasn't too downhearted initially. Hannah would eventually glance at her hand, see her naked finger, realise what she'd done and find me in the bin. But it didn't happen that way.

Three voices and much laughter rang out from the dining room, and I remained wedged between a dried-up garlic clove and a large carrot top all evening. Then, moments after Will and Hannah waved goodbye to their sated guest, Will took it upon himself to empty the indoor compost bin out onto the outdoor compost heap. I believe he muttered something about not wanting the smell of garlic to permeate the house.

Okay, I thought. I'm only 10 feet from the kitchen. Hannah is bound to notice that I'm missing when she's washing her face and cleaning her teeth. She'll panic momentarily, put two and two together and be outside with a torch in moments.

That first night in the compost heap was surprisingly fun. I was certain Hannah would find me in the morning, so I settled down to observe life in the underground mini-city. My two previous owners had both been keen gardeners and I'd picked up a fair amount of compost knowledge over the years – but I had no idea there was quite so much activity! Ants, beetles, centipedes, cockroaches, earthworms, earwigs, flatworms, slugs, snails, woodlice and flies scampered, slid, meandered and burrowed through the heap, feeding, breeding and breaking down the fibrous products like a tiny wildlife army.

At what felt like 7.00 in the morning, the time Will usually left for work, I was aware of Hannah's voice close by. She was chiding herself for losing me and praying she would find me before Will found out. I could feel her sorting through the piles of rotting vegetation, occasionally letting out a squeal at what I presumed was a slimy slug or some other unattractive inhabitant.

With each new dig and sweep, she grew more impatient and upset. While large chunks of cabbage and roots worked their way to the top, smaller, heavier items like stones – and a wedding band – dropped further into the heap. The elation I had felt on feeling her presence also began to drop, and I willed her to adopt a more methodical way of searching.

Suddenly, she stopped, let out an expletive and ran back in the direction of the house. I was aware of a sound out on the road. A sound that would have sealed my fate had Will thrown me in the recycling bin instead of the compost heap. It was the bin lorry with its giant mouth crashing down on old newspapers and compostable bags filled with scraps, peelings and unwanted dinners. If Hannah believed I was in there, I was doomed.

No, I told myself moments later. She wouldn't give up that easily! When Will got home from work, she'd ask him what he did with the contents of yesterday's bin. He'd tell her he'd put it on the compost heap and they'd both be back here this evening to do a thorough search. No problem. I could stay here and enjoy the flora and fauna a little longer.

I actually enjoyed the day, and I grew excited when I heard the early evening birdsong fill the air. Jackdaws squeaked, blackbirds clicked, and a tiny thrush provided a fitting soprano descant.

The delightful sound was suddenly interrupted by an unpleasant noise and a fast movement of soil, plants and creatures. Something large, loud and smelly was sniffing around. Buster. The neighbour's bulldog. An undignified animal with a constant deluge of slimy fluid emanating from its mouth, Buster was swallowing up any edible organic matter on the heap. Ants and flies managed to dodge out of the way, but several woodlice and centipedes found themselves wrapped up in wet cabbage and disappeared down the beast's throat in seconds.

Unable to move or cry out, I willed myself smaller. But it was no good. The large, lapping tongue wrapped around me and I too was scooped up into the dark, wet mouth. A slight crunch, a feeble cough and moments later I was sliding my way down the oesophagus and into the stomach. For the sake of honour and decency, I shall refrain from describing the series of events that took me in, around and out of that hideous brute.

Suffice to say that I welcomed the rain when I eventually emerged into the daylight some days later.

From the familiar sights and sounds around me, I deduced that I was on the back lawn of Mr and Mrs Adeyemi, two doors down. Fortunately, there had been an early morning frost and the ground was frozen solid. Instead of being hidden by the long blades, I was lying on the top of the grass – albeit inside a rather large pile of canine faeces.

Without flies to rid the garden of Buster's waste, I had expected it to be some time before someone noticed me. Not so. Little master Adeyemi had clearly been given a new bicycle and was keen to do 'wheelies' on the unsuitable lawn. Inexperience, frozen grass and sticky poo proved too much for the young lad. The front wheel of the bike slid, and he toppled over in a most undignified fashion.

During all the tears and commotion, Mr Adeyemi stepped on my temporary home, swore loudly and attempted to kick the sticky pile into the shrubbery. The only thing that didn't venture further than the soul of his shoe was me. I landed with a bump under a prickly quince and lay among the rotting fruit. Any happiness I had felt at the likelihood of Hannah finding me in the compost heap had now long gone.

The ground's creatures I'd initially found entertaining now irritated me, especially those who seemed to find amusement crawling through the middle of me. Occasionally, a hedgehog would wander through the garden and feed on sleepy slugs and worms. One particularly large and noisy hedgehog got a little too close to me one evening, but a family of beetles managed to jostle me out of the way just in time. I really don't think I could have survived another digestive experience.

I resigned myself to months, possibly years, in my new home and passed the time imagining all the things Hannah and I would enjoy together when finally reunited.

Then, as luck would have it, a prolific squirrel spent a few weeks procuring a rather large hoard of hazelnuts from a nearby twisted hazel tree and planted several just inches from me. By spring, two of the nuts had burst into life and were growing into small but distinctive saplings. A few small roots of one sampling had found their way inside me and, as the sapling grew in size and strength, I found myself being pushed further down into the soil.

This turned out to be rather fortuitous. Knowing Hannah's interest in gardening, Mrs Adeyemi dug up the little hazel tree and placed me and it into a 9-inch pot. A few hours later, she handed the gift to Hannah. I couldn't believe my luck. I was back where I should be! I was in the hands of my owner – granted there was a thin layer of soil and plastic between us – and as soon as she pulled the little tree out of the pot, she would see me protruding from its roots.

It was a cold spring, so I had to wait a little longer than I hoped to be reunited with my dear lady. She placed me in the greenhouse until the ground warmed up a little. I missed the vibrant life of the garden. But I wasn't complaining. I was warm, safe and only weeks away from being found. Or so I thought.

I guess there's a good reason why the world isn't full of twisted hazel trees. Despite their seeds being spread widely by squirrels, the saplings rarely survive beyond a few feet tall and by the time Hannah returned to plant hers, the little plant had withered and died. I felt a new level of sadness as I heard Hannah gasp. "Well, you won't go entirely to waste," she said, removing the plant from the pot. "All organic matter gratefully received."

She then walked to the newly prepared vegetable patch, tipped the dead sapling upside down and dropped it and me onto the ground. I was there on the surface, gleaming in the daylight!

My pale rose gold must have stood out easily among the dark clumps of soil. Any moment now, Hannah would shriek with delight, and I would be back where I belonged. I wouldn't be at all surprised, I thought, if I didn't become the subject of much dinner party stories for some time afterwards!

However, moments later, Hannah returned with a wheelbarrow of manure and dumped the entire load of top of me. She then carefully raked it, and me, into the ground.

It was a good summer and the carrot, beetroot, onion and courgette seeds Hannah planted grew tall and strong. Occasionally, I'd be jostled and moved as their roots pushed down into the ground, and during at least two autumns, Will pulled me to surface as he harvested a bumper crop. The years had taken their toll on my once rose-coloured metal, and I no longer glistened in the sunlight. He shook me off, and I returned to the stones, sand and earth.

I must have travelled the entire length and breadth of the garden in the years I lay there.

Moved along by moles, worms, mice, digging, sifting, turning and weeding. I even ended up in the sieve one morning, shaken furiously with old roots and dead potatoes, only to be tipped back in again.

The nearest I came to returning to Hannah – other than the time in the hazel sapling pot – was one summer when she was cutting some yellow and pink snap dragons to take into the kitchen.

Buster the dog had long left the neighbourhood, but several cats had moved in and regularly used the garden as their toilet. At first, I'd resented their invasion, but I came to find their digging and burying beneficial in getting closer to the surface. One particular tabby had flicked her back legs with such enthusiasm when carrying out her ablutions, she had sent me several inches into the air, and I ended up on the ground next to the very snap dragons Hannah had bent down to pick.

As Hannah lent forward with her secateurs, her gloved hand touched me. I had suffered so many disappointments over the years, I forced myself not to imagine what would happen next. But nothing could prepare me for the misery I felt when Hannah's little girl (she was now a mother) cried out from the kitchen and Hannah hurried back inside.

When she returned some hours later, another feline friend had done her business and I was now back under the ground.

You'd think that all those years apart, I would have resigned myself to my fate. But I never did. Yes, there were dark days, disappointments and rather unpleasant experiences underground. But I never gave up hope. I never forgot my duty. Each spring would bring another opportunity.

Here I was again, aware of the warming of the ground, happy to believe that this year would be the year we'd be reunited. Spring came. The children played in the garden. Will dug over the vegetable patch. And Hannah sowed the carrot, beetroot, courgette and onion seeds. The days lengthened, the ground warmed up and the roots pushed their way down into the soil. Some tickled as they wound their way around me. One was particularly persistent.

Gradually, as the days turned longer and hotter, the persistent root began to expand inside me. Each day it grew fatter, taken up more of my inside diameter until it filled me completely. I now recognised it as a carrot and wondered how it would survive with my metal digging into it. It simply grew around me and fattened out above and below, like a chubby child in a small rubber ring. It should have felt restrictive and uncomfortable but somehow it didn't, and when the days began to get colder again, I was glad of the carrot's warmth inside me.

Autumn. I could feel the earth around me move and the creatures scurry away, as the metal fork bit into the soil.

In previous years, my shiny surface had taken a few knocks and scratches, so I was grateful for the protection of the carrot this year. Light made its way through the cracks in the soil, and I felt a slight tug. Then another. What was happening? Could I let myself think that I was being pulled upwards? Yes. I was. Someone was pulling at the long, fernlike leaves of my carrot and together we were being pulled out of our dark bed!

I could hear Will's voice compliment Hannah on the size of her harvest as she placed my carrot gently onto her growing crop. "There's some funny shapes as usual," she said, "but there's also some right beauties this year." Oh, how right she was!

We were shaken off and placed in a sack in the garage to keep cool. We lay there for a few weeks, some of our bed fellows not faring as well as others. Mice found their way into the sack, nibbling tiny bites out of many, and leaving their distinctive pungent droppings behind. I hung onto hope.

I could hear the garage door open, and light flew in as Hannah opened the sack. "Oh dear," she said. "I shouldn't have left you out here so long. I think some of you have gone off and may be heading straight for the compost heap."

She separated out the good and bad carrots and I wondered which pile I'd been placed in. Please, please, please, I begged. Don't send me back to the compost heap. Please.

I felt myself being lifted and carried. I could see both the kitchen door and the compost heap up ahead and wondered in which direction I'd be heading.

Hannah turned into the kitchen and placed my pile of carrots on the worktop. "There you go," she said. "Take your pick. We have so many this year, you're more than welcome to have as many as you want."

"Are you sure?" asked a voice I recognised. "I don't want to leave you short." It was Mrs Adeyemi. I was in my old kitchen, and I was about to be taken away again! I could feel her sort through the pile. Again, I was separated from the others. Again, my future rested on fate. Again, I was saved.

"I'll just take these. Thank you. That's more than enough for pakora."

Mrs Adeyemi left with her carrots and Hannah called the children into the kitchen to help prepare dinner. She carried a small step stool to the sink and a little boy climbed up and turned on the cold tap. She then picked me up along with three other carrots, cut off the last of our withering leaves and threw us into the sink.

"Scrub them properly," she said. "Some of those are a bit bruised and rather dirty. We might have to throw some away."

Tiny fingers wrapped themselves around me as another tiny hand picked up a potato brush and began tickling me with it. Cool water trickled down me as the little boy washed away the brown earth.

"Treasure," he cried, as he wiped my carrot against his t-shirt. "I've found buried treasure!"

Hannah was supervising her daughter peeling potatoes and didn't pay much attention to the boy's find. He began to pull at me, trying to free me from the engorged carrot, and accidentally turned the tap on full. Water splashed everywhere, the boy shrieked, and Hannah came over to see what all the fuss was about.

"What are you doing, Tom?" Hannah turned off the tap and gently eased the soaking boy away from the sink. "Here give me that and go and change into something dry."

"It's mine," Tom shouted out. "Give me my treasure!"

"What has Mummy told you about being rude?" Tom was about to protest again when Hannah bent down to take a closer look at the carrot. "Let Mummy see your carrot, sweetheart. I won't keep it. I just want to look."

Taking the still dirty carrot from the boy, she held it up to the light and gasped. "See. Treasure," came the little voice again. Hannah ran the tap again, picked up the brush and wiped the last of the soil off me.

"No. It can't be. Can it? It is. It's my ring. It's my wedding..."

She burst into tears then and both children asked if Mummy was okay. Daddy was called for and when he arrived, she handed him me and the carrot. After he had taken several photos on his phone of all things, Hannah told him the story she'd been keeping from him for over 10 years.

She had realised during dinner that she wasn't wearing her ring, but she hadn't wanted to make a fuss in front of their guest. She'd also been worried about telling Will, so she'd waited until the following morning. When she'd seen the waste collection vehicle, she had begged the bin men to let her look inside, but they refused. Too dangerous. They did, however, take her name and number and promise to call her if anything was found at the site later.

Too embarrassed to confess that she had lost Will's token of their love, she went out during her lunch hour that day, took cash out her savings account and bought a new antique-styled rose gold ring from a High Street jeweller. Broaching the subject of the empty compost bin carefully that evening, Hannah learned that Will had put me on the compost heap. As soon as he left the house the following morning, she went through every inch for over an hour. Of course, I was no longer there. Years passed before she eventually stopped expecting to see me in the compost heap. But she never forgot me.

Tears dried, deception forgiven, Will gently cut into my carrot, removed me from its misshapen body, took the imitation ring from Hannah and placed me back where I belonged. Now, I fitted perfectly. Hannah kissed me and Will simultaneously, and the children groaned.

"I will never take you off again," she said to me, planting another kiss on my slightly damaged surface.

A few days later, several newspaper and television journalists came to the house and took a ridiculous number of photos of me, Hannah, Will, the carrot, the vegetable patch and a different compost bin under the kitchen sink. When our story appeared all over what everyone was calling social media, it said that I must have been scattered onto the vegetable patch in 2009 and had probably lain there undisturbed for 10 years. Undisturbed? Ha! If only I could speak, what a tale I would tell.

Planting primroses in potholes

Linda was waiting for me when PC Gail Ferguson brought me out of the interview room. She had that 'what have you done now, Mother?' look that she gives when she's annoyed but doesn't want others to know.

"She hasn't been arrested or even cautioned," the policewoman explained. I know you're not supposed to call them that nowadays, but old habits die hard. "We've simply asked Mary to stop planting primroses in potholes. She could get seriously hurt by passing traffic. Or endanger other road users."

I wanted to explain that I only ever plant primroses in the quiet side roads, the ones the council doesn't bother about. I wanted to say that what I was doing was less dangerous than having holes in the road.

Only the other week, I'd seen a cyclist go over the handlebars when his bike plummeted into a pothole in Hawthorn Close. But I just nodded dutifully and allowed Linda to sound significantly sorry on my behalf.

A moment or two later, and with a few 'Health and Safety for the Elderly' leaflets in Linda's bag, we were in her flashy BMW heading out of the police station car park.

"Why do you do this, Mum?" Linda said. "Do you enjoy making my life as difficult as possible? I had to walk out of an important meeting to come here. And track down another mum to pick Dana up from school."

"You needn't have rushed over," I said. "It was perfectly pleasant in there. Is Dana all right? Did you find someone to pick her up?"

Linda didn't to want to let me off the hook just yet. She told me I had no understanding of how difficult life was for her. She'd hoped that my moving into Shire House would have made life easier. But no, hardly a day went by without Mrs Curran having to call her about some problem or other.

After suitable admonishment, Linda said that Dana was at a friend's house. "They have a pool," she added, "so she's in her element."

"Good for her," I said, feeling pleased I'd got her a little treat.

It was after six by the time we got back to Shire House and Mrs Curran made it clear I'd missed supper and there wasn't anyone in the kitchen to make a sandwich. Apparently, I'd caused a "right fuss" earlier and she'd had to send the cook home. Linda seemed a bit annoyed about that, so I lied about having some cheese and biscuits in my room.

"Well, if you're sure…" Linda said, getting her car keys out of her handbag. I said I was. Linda gave me a light kiss. Mrs Curran went back to her office, and I took myself off to my room.

As instructed by one of the umpteen laminated leaflets that adorned the walls of Shire House, I'd closed my window when I'd left earlier. My room was now blazing hot, so I opened the window and breathed in the March air. I love the smell of tree blossom in spring.

I wondered if that copy of *Gardeners' World* was still in the lounge. I'd seen an offer for pansies. Maybe they'd make good pothole fillers? After all, I'd only been banned from planting primroses in potholes.

What with the excitement of the day, and missing supper, I didn't sleep much that night. I kept thinking about Linda and how much trouble I cause her. She thinks I do it on purpose. I don't. In fact, I've spent my entire life trying to appease her.

I don't think she's ever forgiven me for having her so late in life. She always seems embarrassed by me. Her dad and I had given up trying to have a baby when I fell pregnant with her. I was 43. Not unusual nowadays, of course. Linda was 37 when she had Dana. But back then, the only older women at the school gates were grandmas. We'd lost six, you see. Something about my placenta breaking up too early. Jack seemed to take it harder than me. Felt responsible for putting me through so much pain.

I'd never seen Jack so happy as he was the day Linda was born. It was like everything he'd ever done in life had been for that moment. He was a marvellous dad. Never minded the mess and the sleepless nights. Never complained about anything, even when I got post-natal depression and couldn't feed her.

All that waiting, and he never even saw her first birthday. Just a few weeks beforehand, his lorry hit a massive pothole up on Mulberry Way, went out of control and hit the railway bridge head on. He'd driven all the way back from Edinburgh and he died half a mile from home. They said it was instantaneous, that he wouldn't have suffered. That was a blessing.

I never did anything about the accident. Never complained to the council about the state of the roads. Never even told Linda. I didn't have time. Or energy. She wasn't the easiest of kids.

It was clear I wasn't going to get any sleep that night, so I got up, found the *Gardeners' World*, tore out the page with the pansies offer, filled in the form and popped it into an envelope along with a cheque.

I knew exactly where I was going to plant them. One of the residents, Billy Webster, had complained about a pothole on Cherry Tree Lane. Said his son had bust a wheel on his Mondeo because of the darned thing. Cost him a small fortune to have it replaced.

I managed to get a bit of sleep after that and woke up surprisingly fresh. I got myself down to breakfast nice and early and tucked into a poached egg, a slice of bacon, two sausages and a bit of toast.

Only it wasn't really toast. It was bread that had been warmed up long enough to produce a gold patch in one corner.

"You're certainly putting it away this morning, Mary," said Billy Webster. "It's not like you to eat much at breakfast." I don't know where he'd got that notion from. He's usually too busy flirting with Mrs Patel to notice what I put in my mouth. "I suppose now you've reached celebrity status, you'll be wanting more than porridge in the mornings."

"What are you on about, Billy Webster?"

"Young lad said there'd be a big piece in The Echo on Thursday," Billy added. "Spoke to a few of us, he did, after you'd be taken away in the police car yesterday. Coming back to see you today, he said."

I was a bit curious, but I didn't want to give him the satisfaction of showing it. So, I finished my tea and headed back to my room. Or at least I tried. Mrs Curran caught me on the way and told me that The Echo had been on the phone – again – and that if I didn't put an end to all this planting primroses nonsense, I might find myself in the hands of Social Services.

"I am not," she said firmly, "having the reputation of Shire House tarnished by the actions of one irresponsible resident!"

Part of me wanted to be the rebel and take my last few primroses up to Cherry Tree Lane right there and then. But they were right. It was time to pack it in. I'd be 86 in July, and it was getting harder to pull my shopping trolley of compost about with me. I'd only started it because I missed my garden so much and they didn't like you "messing about" with the Shire House grounds. (Although, I did deadhead the petunias and busy lizzies when no-one was looking.)

I was just about to throw the pansies offer in the recycling when I heard a bit of a commotion out in reception. I stuck my head out of my door and there was Mrs Curran with some young chap and Billy Webster. They seemed to be talking about me.

I think if Mrs Curran hadn't ordered me back to my room like a naughty toddler, I probably wouldn't have even spoken to Jules, the young chap from The Echo. But I was a bit annoyed by that so when Billy called me the "guerrilla gardener," I said I'd be happy to give Jules five minutes.

We spoke for what seemed like hours. Lovely young chap, he was. Said his grandad was a keen gardener and they'd both been dying to find out who'd been planting the primroses. When his 'source' at the police station said an 85-year woman had been brought in about the pothole business, Jules went straight round for the story. We only stopped nattering because Billy knocked on my door and said that Linda was on the phone.

Linda was livid. The Echo had been hounding her at home and at the office. They wanted to know what it was like having a political campaigner in the family. Political campaigner? Me? I sort of switched off after that. Linda did her usual. Made me feel bad about myself. Made herself feel bad about making me feel bad. Got annoyed again and hung up saying she was "too busy for all of this".

There was indeed a huge spread in the paper on the Thursday. Three photos (one of me in the grounds, one of the potholes in Cherry Tree Lane, and one of my shopping trolley and a tray of primroses that the photographer had brought) and the big headline: "Guerrilla Gardening Pensioner Forces Council Into £250,000 Roads Investment".

I wasn't surprised when Linda turned up at Shire House that lunchtime, brandishing a copy of The Echo. But I was surprised to see her husband Paul and little Dana with her.

"Oh, Mum," Linda said. "Why did you never tell me?"

She wasn't carrying that big laptop case she normally has, and she didn't seem to know what to do with her hands, so I took them in mine, and she gave me a hug. Then Dana hugged me round the waist and Paul moved forward and we all did one of those group hug things where nobody knows when to let go.

I'm not saying that Jules lied about my "life-long campaign against potholes" but he certainly embellished the truth about Jack being killed in 1975 and me being "carted off by several officers" on Tuesday morning. I'd never made the connection between my pothole filling and Jack's accident. Or maybe I had, subconsciously.

It was nice being a celebrity for a couple of weeks. A few of the nationals picked up the story and I was even "trending on Twitter" for a day or two.

But life went back to normal. Linda brought Dana round at the weekends. The council started filling in the potholes and Mrs Curran gave me one of the Shire House borders to maintain.

A good month or so after all the hoo-ha died down, Linda popped in one Saturday morning. We went through the usual "what did you have for dinner last night" routine and then she stood up and looked out the window.

"It can't have been easy for you," she said, still with her back to me. "Bringing me up on your own, taking me with you when you cleaned the doctor's surgery in the evenings."

She turned around and I could see her eyes filling up. "I'm so sorry, Mum. I was ashamed. I told people you were a nurse... Now I tell them you're the lady who planted primroses in potholes. The lady I'm proud to call my mother."

We had a little cry then and said a few things we'd both been wanting to say for years. Then we dried our eyes and got back to safe subjects like what I wanted for my birthday and wasn't Dana getting tall.

We're thinking of starting one of those urban food gardens, Linda and I, on that patch of ground up by the school. Get the kiddies growing veg.

Who knows? Maybe, I'll give Jules a ring. I'm sure he's always looking for a good story.

Snowflakes and hailstones

I wasn't sure what was bothering me more. Fearing I was going to die a slow painful death. Or having Grant tell me he was right.

Being alone in a 23-year-old Mazda at four twenty on a February morning with little or no petrol and 112 miles from civilisation was probably enough of a punishment without worrying about Grant's face. Add in the fact that I was now on roads that hadn't been serviced for over 10 years, and dangerously close to The Settlement, it was surprising how remarkably perky I felt. Maybe I was a good journalist after all?

"143 miles," I'd said to Grant. "It's only 143 miles. I mean, seriously, how long can it take to drive 143 miles? Okay. I know it's not like before. I know I'm going to have to avoid the motorways. Probably the dual carriageways, too. But even taking the B-roads, we're talking, what, three hours? Four max? It's nothing, is it? God, Mum and Dad used to drive all the way to Carlisle in time for breakfast!"

The words that had sounded so right, so strong, in my head, now fell like wet snow as I said them out loud to Grant.

"143 miles there," he'd replied. "286 miles there and back. And don't tell me the fuel consumption on that old banger is phenomenal because achieving an average 46 miles to the gallon is the least of your worries."

"But he's my grandad," the melting snowflakes had pleaded. "My only living relative. I can't just leave him up there. I can't. I won't."

"He's 88, Cassie. Old. Frail. He could be dead already, for all you know."

I pushed the pile of wet slush around with my foot. "All the more reason to go today, then."

Grant was right. It was a ludicrous notion. Grandad could be dead. Why did I think I could succeed where Mum and Dad had failed? Grant was always right. But I hadn't been able to get through on the phone to Grandad for weeks and the security cameras Dad had installed back in 2029 had stopped working three days ago. Whatever food the last carer had left for him months ago would either have been eaten by now or have gone off. And if the phone and cameras weren't working, there was a pretty good chance he had no heat, light or water either. Realistically, what were the chances he was still alive?

But the journalist in me took over again. The adrenaline returned, my heartbeat increased, and I pressed the start button as the Mazda chugged grudgingly into life.

Keeping on the side lights only to avoid alerting The Settlement, I pulled out of the lay-by and drove on. The fuel gauge was still on three quarters of a tank. At least I'd been right about that.

"You know I would come with you but…" Grant's parting words had made my pile of pathetic snowflakes seem like an avalanche. I hadn't even bothered to listen to what came after 'but'. It was irrelevant. I knew he was no good for me. No good for each other. But when you have no one else in your life, it's easy to stay anchored in the wrong port.

Dad had explained The Big Divide to me when I was very young, but I'd never really understood it. Apparently, when Dad was a kid, the whole country had been relatively prosperous. The taxes created by oil, manufacturing, farming, technology, financial and medical research had benefitted the regions where there was less work, and the more affluent areas had supported the Needies with something called Social Services.

But the more the Hard-Workers supported the Needies, the less the Needies did. Eventually, there were more sick, old, disabled, unemployed and (according to Dad) lazy people than Hard-Workers and Social Services collapsed. Anyone outside of the City was left to "make do". Those in the City who had the wherewithal to get out, went to the Regions to bring families and friends back to the City. But most of them perished on the way there or the way back.

It had been over two years since Mum and Dad had left. My eyes misted up again, but I pushed the memory back. The last thing I needed now was sentimentality.

Driving through the night was difficult enough. Driving with side lights only was making it almost impossible to stay awake.

Shit! What the fuck was that? A loud rumbling sound cut into my thoughts, and I braked involuntarily. I checked the rear view and side mirrors. Nothing. I peered into the darkness. Nothing. Then, wham! Something slammed into the back of the car and shunted me into the side of the road. I narrowly missed a tree, skidded and stopped abruptly in a pile of mud and leaves.

"Get out of the car!" a male voice screamed at me. "Get the fuck out of the car!" Standing in front of the Mazda was a scrawny creature with what can only be described as wild eyes. "Get the fuck out of the car now or I'll rip you from it limb by limb!"

He began yanking at the door handle. Thank heavens I'd had the sense to lock the door. He slammed what must have at one time been a boot into the door. Then he picked up a nearby branch and smashed it into the windscreen.

I'd often wondered how I'd react when threatened with my life. I remember watching scary movies with Dad when I was a kid, hiding behind him and several cushions with my eyes firmly shut. "Tell me when it's stopped," I'd say. Dad would laugh, tell me it had stopped, and I'd peak out from behind him in time to see someone having their stomach ripped open. I'd squeal. Dad would shriek with laughter and promise, Big Dad Promise, not to do that again. It was years before I stopped falling for it.

Now, as this gangly young man with wild eyes was yelling and cursing at me, I was surprised at how calm I felt.

Wham! One final swing and the cracked windscreen split open, sending cubes of powder blue glass flying all over me. I screamed. I screamed so loudly that Gangly Body actually backed off. "Get the fuck out of the fucking, cunting car," he spat. I resisted the urge to explain the difference between nouns, verbs and adjectives, and turned myself into a hedgehog, the blue cubes of glass making a feeble effort to be my spines.

Cowered under the steering wheel, I could feel his bony hands clawing at me, yanking at my hair, pulling at the hood of my Barbour. The studs popped and the hood slipped off. I looked up and saw the wild eyes burn red. Then there was a gunshot and the eyes widened as blood and brains burst out of the tiny head. Another shot rang out and the fur trim on my Barbour hood adorned itself with globs of human parts.

I think I must have passed out at that point because the next thing I was aware of was another male voice grunting and cursing as the car rocked its way out of the ditch. I didn't know how I'd ended up in the passenger seat or who or what was moving the car. I felt as if I was watching a scene from a film, a scene I'd been in some time ago yet was watching it play out now. The scene ran on a loop as time moved between standing still and running backwards. The car suddenly jolted forwards, halted, and the driver's door flew open. A man about my age got in, sparked up the engine and reversed the Mazda out of the mud heap.

"I'd rather you just killed me now," said a voice not dissimilar to my own. "Or I can do it myself, if you prefer."

"Shut up and keep down," the man barked at me. "If they see a woman in the car, we're both dead meat. Literally. What do you think these people live on?"

"Are you one of them? Did you kill the skinny guy? What arc you – "

"Stop asking questions. I need to concentrate."

I didn't know what was happening but something in the man's demeanour was reassuring. So, I allowed myself to obey as he backed out of the woods and onto the road I'd been on what felt like both moments and hours ago.

"Hey," I said, braving a peak out of the car. "Where are you going? You're going the wrong way. Hey! Listen to me – "

"Jesus. Don't you ever give it a rest? I wasn't exactly expecting your hand in marriage as a thank you for saving your life, but a bit of gratitude wouldn't be out of order."

I put the scene together and realised who'd killed the crazy wild eyes guy. I resisted the urge to say, "I would have managed on my own" and grunted a begrudging thank you before continuing my line of questioning.

"Can I at least ask your name?"

"Will. I'm Will. And you?"

"Cassie. But why are we – "

"So, let me guess Cassie, you're a rookie journalist getting nowhere so you're up here trying to get a good story so your editor will take you seriously. Mummy and Daddy refused to let you use the Tesla, so you've nicked Gran's old Mazda, stocked up with an abundance of provisions and are having yourself a real Old Fashioned Adventure."

"Did anyone ever tell you that you're an arrogant little shit?"

"Yes, the last three women I saved from being raped and eaten." He looked at me then. Looked at me properly for the first time. And grinned.

"Okay. I am a journalist. But that has nothing to do with why I'm here. So, thank you for saving my life but if you could please stop the car, I'd like to resume my journey. In the other direction."

"No way. You think that guy was the only one around here? There are hundreds of them in these woods – all laying low, waiting to pounce on the first stupid Do-gooder with food and wheels."

Will drove seriously, watching the road ahead, beside and behind him. He knew the back roads and we were back in safe territory within moments. He glanced at me now and then as he explained how he too had been waiting for a way out. Now that he had my car, there was no way he was giving it up. He was heading south whether I liked it or not. If I was still mad enough to want to venture back to Region 7 once we'd got back to the city, he wouldn't stop me.

"No," I said, strongly. My words might have fallen like snowflakes with Grant, but they tumbled out like hailstones now, each one bigger, rounder and harder than the last. This was my fucking car, I told Will, and unless he was prepared to kill me too, he had better turn round right now and help me rescue my grandfather. "It will make a change from rescuing dumb city damsels," I added. Will bit the side of his mouth, considered my option momentarily and turned the car round silently.

The tension temporarily resolved, Will and I chatted as easily as two singletons on a second date. I told him about Mum and Dad's failed attempts to rescue family and friends. I was surprised to find myself crying. "Sorry," I said. "No-one's interested in anyone else's grief."

"Hey," Will said, touching my arm. "It's okay. Just because we've all lost people, doesn't mean to say it doesn't hurt."

Will told me he'd been a medical student in Region 8 when the government had pulled funding from every district north of Region 3.

Like thousands of others, he had failed to get south before the last trains, planes and buses were stopped from operating in the north. So, he'd stolen a car, and his flatmate, a former soldier who refused to leave, got hold of enough weaponry for Will to stay alive for the best part of a year.

"When I ran out of fuel," Will explained. "I started to walk. But there's only so many nutters you can shoot before you realise there's more of them than there are of you."

Will needed a car with a full tank. He tapped the dashboard. "You've still got over half a tank but we're at least 40 miles from Region 7, plus around 300 miles back to the – "

"300? What do you mean, 300? I worked it out. It's less than 300 there and back."

"Yeah, on the roads. There are Settlements along all the major roads; they'll hijack anything that comes close. We're going to have to take the long route back." Will tapped the dash again. "I hope this old baby's fuel consumption is as phenomenal as you say it is."

It was getting light by the time we got to Grandad's, an old farmhouse a few miles south of what had been Penrith. Unlike the big towns and cities, which now looked like war zones, Grandad's village looked exactly how I remembered it. The post office, pub and corner shop had closed long before the Abandonment.

Yet faded posters and notices still clung to filthy windows by fragile pieces of yellowing tape. Gardens were overgrown with weeds and wildflowers, and, for a moment, I felt a surge of happiness remembering playing outside with my brother and sister, while Mum sat on the front step drinking a mug of tea and telling us to "play nicely".

"Hey! Easy," Will said as I rushed out of the car and pushed open Grandad's gate. "You don't know who's around here." Will got out of the car slowly, shotgun in hand, looking around for any signs of danger. He put his finger to his mouth and walked in front of me. He opened Grandad's front door slowly and beckoned me in.

A tiny man, in filthy clothes, was sitting in Grandad's chair by the fireplace. The smell of decaying food, damp and faeces was overwhelming. I hoped he was just asleep. "Grandad," I said, quietly. "Grandad. It's me. Cassie."

"Hello, Pet," the tiny man said through paper thin lips. "It's lovely to see you. Let me put the kettle on." Even Will seemed to choke back a tear as Grandad made a futile effort to stand.

"It's okay, Grandad. We don't have time for tea. We have to get you out of here."

"No, no. I'm not going out on a day like this. I'm fine here watching the TV." Will and I looked at the old set in the corner, the only picture it showed was a thick layer of oily smoke and dust. "Emmerdale's on tonight."

Grandad's dementia had always been a form of comfort to me when I could watch him on the cameras and talk to him on the phone. It didn't matter that he didn't know what day it was or that it had been 15 years since Gran died. He was happy in his world. A carer would come round once or twice a day, bathe him, bring him a hot meal, and buy him coffee, milk and cakes. It didn't matter that the only programmes on TV were ones from 20 years ago or that the radio played the same 15 songs on a loop. In his world, every minute lasted a day, and every day lasted a minute.

"Hello, Pet," Grandad said, his inflection identical to earlier. "It's lovely to see you. Let me put the kettle on."

"Sir," Will said, battling with breathing through his mouth and speaking at the same time. "We need to get out of here now. We need to get south of the last settlement before dark."

"I'm sorry," Grandad said, his voice almost inaudible. "I can't... remember your name. I never forget... a face but..."

"Grandad!"

"It's okay," Will said, lifting Grandad from the chair. "He's only passed out. But we need to get some fluid into him pronto. I'll take him out to the car. You go round the house. Find anything to eat, drink. Anything. And blankets. Shake off whatever's been shitting on them and take them with you."

Will put Grandad in the back of the car while I gathered up some tins of peaches and soup. I turned on the taps but after a grunt and a trickle of brown liquid, nothing came out. I opened the warm fridge, pushed aside lumps of mould and gagged on a carton of milk.

A bottle of orange juice with a 'use by' date from two months ago had turned alcoholic but it was better than nothing.

"Come on," Will urged me. "I've been upstairs and grabbed these." He was holding my old duvet cover and pillow. The faded cartoon animals etched more on my mind than in the weave. "Everything else is in shreds. The rats must have got to them."

Back in the car, I sat with Grandad in the back, holding the duvet around him as I forced tiny drops of orange vodka into his mouth. "He just keeps bringing it back up again," I said.

"I know. It's the body's reaction to having had nothing for days, possibly weeks. Keep trying."

The second date conversation we'd enjoyed on the way up was replaced by concentrated silence. Will drove us through fields, woods, gardens and dirt tracks. He let out the odd profanity as the car hit a hole, fence or bump. Grandad remained unconscious but breathing. Gradually, I managed to get about 100 mls of liquid into him.

By nightfall, we were just a mile outside the City and Will stopped the car. "You going to be okay from here?"

"What? Why? You're not – "

"I don't have papers. They won't let me in."

"But I thought... No, you have to..."

Will got out of the car and told me to get into the driving seat. "Cover your grandfather up as you drive through the check point. Fortunately, he's so tiny, they'll only see the cover. And dump your coat here or they'll start asking questions about the blood. No. Don't say it. I'll be fine. Go. Go on!"

Again, my words became snowflakes as I pleaded with Will to come with me. I'd say he was my boyfriend, that we'd lost his papers on a day out but my employers, a well-known social media platform, would vouch for him. He thanked me, wished me well and walked away.

"Will!" I screamed as I watched his body disappear into the distance. "Will! I think he's dead. Will. Grandad's dead."

I ran after Will, shouting at him to stop, tripping over cracks and holes in the road. "Will!"

He stopped and turned, his eyes raging with anger and brimming with tears. "Are you fucking crazy? I'm a liability. You know that."

"Grandad didn't make it," I sobbed. "He didn't make it, Will. He's frozen and white and... Grant was right. You were right. I'm stupid and naive and a drama queen... and... If I lose you too, the whole thing will have been for nothing."

Will's snowflakes were as delicate as mine. His protestations melted the moment I reached up and kissed his warm mouth.

"How can you expect snow to settle," I said, "when it comes from a place as warm as you?"

"You are fucking crazy." Will smiled and kissed the tip of my nose. "You know what could happen if you try to smuggle me in?"

I knew. Everyone knew. They made it clear on TV, on social, on billboards. "But if we get away with it, maybe I'll get a chance to write that big story after all?"

We hugged then. And cried. For Grandad. For Dad. For Mum. For my little brother and sister. For grandads and dads and mums and brothers and sisters and cousins and friends everywhere. For the tens of thousands who had perished because they lived 'up north' or risked the journey there. And then we ran back to the 23 year old Mazda with its phenomenal fuel consumption – and cried some more.

The Red Right Hand

I'm neither asleep nor awake. I'm falling backwards into a long, deep blackness. The sensation is not unpleasant. I continue to fall, the dark void swallowing me whole. A small hand reaches out and grabs me. A child's hand. My hand. I see my eight-year-old self. Hear the Aberdonian accent of my childhood. And my head explodes.

"We're on the kitchen floor," the child says. "Da is on his hands and knees and Ma is lying next to him. I must have dropped my paint box because everything is red and sticky. Da's fingers are pressing into arms. He's shouting at me. His face is so close, his spit lands on my lips but I'm too scared to wipe it off."

I wake with a small yelp and see David beside me, smiling. "You okay?" he asks. "Another bad dream?" I nod, get out of bed and change into a dry t-shirt. "You don't have to go through with this, Rachel. You know that, don't you?"

"I do," I say. "I need to see him die."

David insists on coming with me to the Secure Unit. He wants to take my hand, to reassure me, but he knows that I rarely grant anyone permission to touch me. I look into his concerned eyes, and my chest aches for him. He didn't deserve to fall in love with a stone.

A woman of indiscernible years greets us. "Rachel, dear," she says. "I'm Yvonne, your PACT Case Manager. I work for the Prison Advice and

Care Trust." She speaks in the same public sector voice that filled my childhood. "The door will stay open the whole time you're in there. And I'll be right outside with two prison officers. Right here. Okay?" I nod and it seems to make her happy. Then I smile at David, more for his sake than mine.

It's been 30 years since I saw my father. 30 years since the female police officer (we called them policewomen back then) prised me away from Ma's body. 30 years since Da had been given a life sentence for Ma's murder. And 30 years since Social Services had given me a new identity.

"He is still with us," Yvonne adds. "But we don't know for how much longer. The… cancer… it's… spread to his lungs. Stay for as long or as little as you…"

Her voice trails away as I enter the room. I back off almost immediately. The smell of decaying flesh makes me heave. I move towards the body on the bed. It lays on its back, the left hand cuffed to the rail, the right connected to tubes and machines that bleep and click in time with the wheezing of its chest. There is nothing about the grey, lifeless form I recognise.

The body looks much older than its 56 years, but for as long as it breathes, it's still capable of hurting me. "Wake up, you bastard," I say. "Wake up so I can see your eyes and beat the last breath of life out of you."

A withered, white-haired head turns towards me. I draw back instinctively. "Julie? Is that you?"

The voice is terrifyingly familiar.

My hand rises to my mouth, and I force myself to stop gagging. "I'm Rachel," I tell myself. "Rachel. You murdered Julie when you murdered her mother."

"Julie. Come…here… I asked… to see you..." The cuffed hand clenches and stretches; the prize fighter ready to lash out. I try to turn, to flee, to yell for David but my body freezes, my legs buckle, and my eight-year-old self catches me before I hit the ground.

"We're going to a caravan in Arbroath," the child tells me. "We're going to buy a rubber dinghy and eat fish and chips on the beach. Da bought me a colouring book and pencils at the garage and I drew a picture of a bucket and spade. But I must have done the picture wrong because when I showed it to Ma, the book got snatched from my hands and the pencils got snapped in half and we didn't go to the caravan or have fish and chips on the beach."

"Thank you… for coming," he says, the Aberdeen accent as strong as it was 30 years ago. "I didnae want to die…withoot…You need to ken the truth…"

The eyes, pale blue like mine, implore me to listen. But the memories enrage me more than I ever believed possible.

Da's been coming into my room a lot since I drew the bad pictures. He put a lock on my door. Ma keeps thumping on it and crying all night.

Da says I have to stay quiet or things will get worse.

A long, terrifying wail breaks out of my throat. Yvonne and the officers burst into the room. They try to ease me away from the pale blue eyes that now dare to brim with tears. "No, no." I gasp, pulling away from them. "I need to… I need to finish this."

They back off slowly, allowing me to move closer to the bed. I look first at the eyes, too large on the thin, wizened face. Then the neck, grey and scrawny like an old hen. Then the chest, still rising and falling, still capable of filling that sick, dying body with life. And then I see something else, and I drop like lead to the floor, the child too late to catch me this time.

I hear someone call my name. There is commotion outside. Someone is calling for a doctor. Someone else is lifting me up and carrying me out of the room. David is shouting "I'll kill the bastard." Yvonne is urging me to breathe, breathe, take it easy, hush, hush.

I force myself to remain conscious, to speak, to ask, to reason. Words battle in my mouth, but my lips and tongue won't form the right shapes and my thoughts rage in my head like a caged animal throwing itself against the bars.

A doctor, I presume he is a doctor, kneels beside me and places two fingers on my neck. He looks at his watch and the world goes silent. His dark chocolate voice and huge hands sooth and relax me and gradually the words I'd locked away 30 years ago form like clues in front of me. Slowly, I reshape them into the sentences, paragraphs and chapters I'd forced myself to forget.

I'm eight years old, back in our house in Logie Place, hiding in my room. My door is locked but I can't stop the noise seeping in. I get under the covers and try to stop the noise. But it doesn't stop. It gets louder.

I get out of bed and tiptoe to my door. I pull back the lock and open the door far enough to see down into the kitchen. I creep down the stairs. I see them, words and fists lashing out, the soup in the pan boiling over, the table and stool lying on their sides.

A hand knocks the pan of soup on the floor. Another hand turns the knob on the cooker and flames rise into the air. I scream so hard the lining of my throat burns hotter than the flames. I beg for them to stop. To turn off the heat. To take the hand away. But the hand pushes the other closer to the hob and the agonised screams drown out my own.

The hand is held onto the flames and a smell of pork fills my nostrils. The kitchen stool is still on its side, inches from the legs that pin the jerking body against the cooker. The hand quivers on the fire and the screams are so loud I close my eyes tight and cover my ears with my hands. My eyes are closed but I still see the hands. I push my nose into my jumper, but I still smell the pork. I beat my hands against my ears, but I still hear the screams. I rock and cry and shout and beg.

Make it stop. Make it stop. Make it stop. Then another sound, a scarier sound than anything I've ever heard before, drowns out the screams and I open my eyes. I see a hand reaching out for the stool. But before the hand can get to it, a booted foot thumps into the side of my head and I curl up and whimper like a puppy.

The hand reaches out again and manages to get hold of the stool. It drags the stool squealing along the floor and thumps it into one of the legs by the cooker. Another leg lashes out and the stool splits in two, sending splinters flying through the air and Ma's body crashing to the ground. I watch as the stool slams into her face. Again and again, it smashes into her until her head pops open and her brains spill out.

Yvonne's voice breaks into my thoughts. "Rachel? Rachel? Are you okay?"

"Yes," I say. And I realise I am.

"You're not going back in there," David growls. "I won't let you!"

"No," I say, calmly. "I know everything now. I need to see him one last time."

I draw up a chair beside him. He reaches out to me. He looks like a wounded animal, the blue eyes terrified, the mouth gaping, beads of sweat on the paper-thin skin of his forehead. I realise that I must now look exactly like my mother. I take hold of the hand and he winces. "It's okay," I say. "I'm Julie. Your Julie."

I stroke the skin on the palm of his right hand and my heart splits in two. Unlike the translucent grey of his face and arms, the burnt flesh on the right hand is a dark rust red. "Thank you," I whisper.

We're on the kitchen floor. Da is on his hands and knees and Ma is lying next to him. Da's fingers are pressing into my arms. He's shouting at me. His face is so close, his spit lands on my lips. "Da's going to fix this, okay? You're going to tell the Bobbies what we practised, okay? Let me hear you say it."

"Ma held Da's hand on top of the flame and I picked up the stool..."

"No, pet. Da picked up the stool. Say it. Say, 'I saw Da pick up the stool. I saw Da hit Ma over the head.' Say it. Say it, Julie."

I remembered the sound the moment I saw his hand. The other sound I'd heard in the kitchen that night. Not the flames. Not the screaming. Not the stool I slammed against my mother's head. But the jeering, mocking, shrilling sound of her demonic laughter.

I want to speak, to say sorry, to thank him for protecting me, to beg him to forgive me, to explain that I'd pushed the truth so far back, I'd come to believe our concocted story. But his eyes silence me, his almost imperceptible nod warning me to keep the faith just a little longer.

I hold his red right hand long after they take out the tubes and silence the machines.

David joins me and I smile. "Are you ready?" he asks, his voice so quiet I see rather than hear the words. "Are you ready to leave?"

"No," I say, touching Da's arm. "I'm ready to start."

Ten thousand hours of ignorance

Thursday 23 October 2014

Irene McDonald walked out of the Old Bailey to a barrage of questions from journalists. "Is this the verdict you expected?" "What happens now, Ms McDonald?" "What do you say to the two police forces and three home secretaries that tried to shut you up?"

***

Friday 25 June 2004

Irene recognised the desk sergeant's type right away. Middle aged. Tired. Putting in the hours until he could collect his final salary police pension.

"And he goes away a lot, you say?" He made it sound more like an explanation than a question.

"Yes. But I always know where he is. And he always calls me." Irene tried to keep the frustration out of her voice.

"And his mobile just goes to voicemail, you say?"

"No." Irene breathed deeply. "I get a message saying the number hasn't been recognised."

"Could be all sorts of explanations." His weariness was testing her resolve. "Why don't we leave it for a day or two, eh? See if…" He looked at his notes. "See if… Andy… gets in touch."

Irene tried a few more approaches but, worried she'd get hysterical, she settled for a 'missing persons' leaflet and a promise to come back Monday. First thing.

It was after eleven by the time she'd got back to her flat. She never gave herself the luxury of leaving the heating on, but she wished she'd at least left a light on. She'd been out since six, checking his gym, his regular drinking haunts, hoping somebody might have heard something. Hoping to avoid exactly what had happened at the police station. She checked her mobile again. Nothing.

As she walked into the living room, she noticed a red light flashing in the darkness. Had he called the landline? Darting over to listen to the message, she banged her shin on the coffee table and cursed. "It won't be him," she told herself, hitting the button. "Don't get your hopes up. It won't be him."

"Irene. It's mum." Her hopes fell like a heavy bag of flour. "I'm sure you haven't forgotten… but just in case… your dad and I are really looking forward to seeing you and Andy on Sunday." She sat down on the floor, rubbed her shin and gave into tears.

A large glass of wine and an episode of Film 2004 sent her into a fitful sleep. She dreamt about a camping trip she and Andy had gone on with her brother Tom not long after they'd met last year. Only, in the dream, it wasn't a tent; it was her old bedroom. And it wasn't Andy she was with; it was her first boyfriend, Paul. And Andy/Paul was laughing and kicking Tom in the stomach.

***

Saturday 26 June 2004

She woke up sobbing from the dream, her neck stiff from falling asleep on the sofa. She forced herself to get up, think straight, do something positive. If the police weren't going to help, she'd have to do something herself.

She'd go to his office. She wasn't sure where it was – she'd never actually been there – but she was sure she'd seen an address lying around on a worksheet. Andy often worked Saturdays. Maybe there'd be somebody there this morning and there'd be a simple explanation for all of this?

She should ring Tom. She hadn't wanted to worry him yesterday, hadn't wanted to make a big thing of it. She'd hoped Andy would have called by now, said he'd broken his phone, been stuck in a traffic in France or something. She'd even been prepared for a call from a hospital. "As long as he's not dead", she told herself. There had to be a logical explanation. It was only a day, after all. This time next week, they'd be laughing about it.

Andy always said she was overdramatic, overthought everything. He took life in his stride. It was one of the things she'd found attractive about him when they'd met fourteen months ago.

She'd been doing her master's in politics at Reading University and working part-time at the

Hare & Hounds near Reading Station. Andy had come in with a group of jocks from the nearby gym.

***

Thursday 10 April 2003

It wasn't that he was taller or better looking than the other guys. It was the way they listened to him that fascinated her. She didn't need to hear men's conversations to know what they were talking about. She could see it. The pointing, the thrusting, the interrupting. The laughing longer than necessary.

But he didn't do any of that. He didn't push. He drew them in. Everything about him was slow. Deliberate. He would hold his pint to his mouth momentarily before sipping it. He would open his mouth to speak then pause for a second. He would laugh for just the right length of time.

She was serving two women who couldn't decide what wine they wanted when he appeared in front of her. "You're Irene, aren't you?" His Belfast accent was softer than the ones she was used to. "Tom's sister. He said you worked here."

"How do you know Tom?" she asked, glancing at the two women. They seemed no closer to deciding.

"Met him at the 'Stop the War' march in February."

"Tom? Are you sure?" Irene laughed then apologised. "Sorry. But my brother can barely make it out of bed to get a coffee in the morning. I can't imagine him on a peace protest!"

"In fairness, he was more interested in finding a Costa and chatting up the women." He paused. "Looks like you're wanted."

"What?"

"Your ladies. They've settled on cider."

Irene gave the women Magners on ice then served a stream of after-work drinkers and stag parties before she got the chance to talk to Andy again. He'd recently moved to Reading from Ballymena (not Belfast) and was working as a long-distance lorry driver. Temporarily. To help out a mate. He'd only gone on the march himself because of growing up during The Troubles.

A couple of weeks passed before Irene saw Andy again. In the intervening period, she'd quizzed Tom about the march and, more to the point, the guy from Northern Ireland.

Tom could barely recall Andy, but he clearly remembered an American girl he'd got off with, a member of some animal/human/environmental rights group. "Which was it?" Irene had asked. "God knows," Tom had said. "But she had great tits."

***

Friday 2 May 2003

"So, what do you recommend?" She'd almost forgotten how gorgeous his accent was. She poured him a taster from the pub's microbrewery, and they went back to her flat four hours later.

She'd never had sex with anyone that quickly before. She thought she'd be furious with herself in the morning, that he'd bugger off and she'd never see him again. But it wasn't like that. He wasn't like that. Everything about their relationship, about him, was easy.

He moved in with her three weeks later, his few boxes of books and protein shakes as manageable as he was. Friends and family loved him, the temporary driving job turned into a permanent one and Irene got used to cramming in essays when he was away so they could spend all day together when he got back.

***

Saturday 26 June 2004

Now, he was gone. He hadn't been in the flat when she'd got back from Uni yesterday. No note. No call. No word since. Nothing in his behaviour over the past year or so had given Irene the slightest indication he'd just walk out on her. It was no good. She called Tom.

"Sorry," Tom said, as Irene let him into the flat two hours later. "I left as quickly as I could but even this early, the traffic is – " Irene fell into his arms and sobbed.

Half an hour later, they pulled up outside Andy's office, a shabby under-the-arches unit in an industrial estate near Maidenhead. "You sure this is it?" Tom asked, getting out of the Mazda. "Looks a bit dead."

Irene rang the bell and Tom peered in through the window. "That's odd," Tom said. "No computer. No papers. Just a desk and a wardrobe. Why's there a wardrobe in an office?"

"He doesn't like coming home smelly after a long drive." Irene's explanation sounded feeble.

Tom got some tools from his car and forced the office door open. It was radical but Irene was desperate. The office felt unlived in, cold and musty. Tom checked the desk drawers while Irene looked in the wardrobe. A leather jacket hung from the rail. Two shirts, some jeans and a washbag lay on the shelf. She went through the jacket pockets. Three photos fell to the floor.

The top one was of her and Andy, taken at her parent's house at Christmas. The second was of a fair haired toddler running towards a blonde woman, presumably his mother. The third was of Andy with his arm around a large breasted woman with short red hair and an earring through her nose. She handed them to Tom and leant against the desk to steady herself.

"What the…" Tom looked at the red haired woman. "I know her. It's Kristen, the bird I met on the march last year."

"Are you sure?"

"Oh yeah. You don't forget those babies in a hurry." Irene ran outside and threw up.

They drove back to her flat, Irene in silence, Tom apologising for his callousness. "They were probably taken years ago," he offered. "Maybe they're his sister and nephew." A sister and nephew he'd never mentioned.

At Tom's insistence, Irene had a shower and a mouthful of toast. "You have to remember something other than her breasts," Irene said, pushing crumbs around her plate.

"I... I might have a vague idea of the house we went back to."

They drove to Raynes Park in southwest London. The traffic was abysmal, and it was early evening by the time they got to a street Tom sort of recognised.

"What are you even going to say?" Tom asked, as they walked up to a house with an overgrown garden and filthy net curtains. The front door was covered in faded stickers – 'Stop bombing Iraq.' 'Blair – liar and murderer'.

"Looks like we've got the right place," Irene said, banging on 'No blood for oil'.

A dog barked, someone called out and the door opened to reveal a pale, skinny boy of about 15. He was wearing pyjama bottoms and nothing else. Irene froze.

"Hi," Tom said. "We're friends of Kristen. Is she around?"

"Who?"

"Kristen. Show him the picture, Irene."
Irene's hand shook as she passed the boy the photo.

"Never seen her before," the boy said,
returning the photo.

"Please." Irene moved in to stop the door
closing.

"What the fuck do you want?" A big man in
track suit bottoms and a vest came out of the
kitchen. The boy slid away.

"Hey." Tom forced his voice down a tone or
two. "Sorry to bother. We're looking for Kristen.
Wanted to surprise her."

"She's gone," the big man said. "Went back
to the States after that bastard fucked off." The man
pointed to the photo in Irene's hand.

"You know Andy?" Irene asked, her voice
barely audible.

"Andy? Who the fuck's Andy. That's
Callum. The fucking grass."

Back in the car, Irene and Tom tried to make
sense of what the big man had said. "He's probably
off his head on something," Irene reasoned. "His
Callum probably just looks a bit like my Andy."

"He seemed pretty lucid to me."

"I mean, come on, Tom. Do you honestly
believe Andy is an undercover policeman? Andy?"

"I don't know…He seemed to describe
Andy… Callum… pretty well…But no. Course
not… Only…"

"What?"

"Well, Kristen was – well they all were – a bit, you know, subversive."

"Okay, okay. So, let's say this Callum guy was a cop and he was investigating Kristen. Why would Andy be investigating me?"

None of it made sense but, with no other way of checking, they went back to the police station.

Last night's desk sergeant had been replaced with an impossibly young looking female. She seemed to find the notion of an undercover policeman having relationships with women connected to subversive groups both implausible and exciting.

"I'll take over from here, Constable." A man in his fifties approached and introduced himself as Superintendent Paul Davis. He suggested Tom and Irene join him in his office.

He was polite, sympathetic and in no doubt there was no truth in their suggestion. "I'm sorry, Irene," he said, leading them out. "Sometimes we let hurt cloud our judgement. I strongly suggest you put all this behind you and get on with life."

***

Friday 24 October 2014

The Metropolitan Police agreed to pay £425,000 to a woman who didn't know the father of her child was an undercover policeman.

She was the blonde woman in the photo Irene and Tom had found on that Saturday morning in June 2004.

It had taken Irene eight years of being fobbed off and threatened by the police to finally discover the truth. Working with a group of women who claimed the police had used sex to infiltrate their groups, she eventually found out that Andy was Michael O'Shea.

Michael O'Shea had worked for the Metropolitan Police, had been married and had had at least three relationships with women 'connected' to subversive organisations. When intelligence revealed that Tom wasn't involved with the Raynes Park group, Irene no longer served a purpose and Michael was called to another project. He was now living in Australia under a new identity.

As she left the court with five other women, Irene stopped by the impatient paparazzi, waited for their questions to quieten and took a deep breath. "This is just the start," she said. "A bloody good start. But, make no mistake, it is just the start."

Printed in Great Britain
by Amazon

21901181R00088